# THE SCULPTURES

And other Short Plays

Originally written in Tamil by
**AR. Arul Selvan**

Translated by
**Andrew Joseph**

Edited by
**Mohamed**
**TransCloud Language Services**
Chennai

NOTION PRESS

NOTION PRESS

India. Singapore. Malaysia.



Published Year: 2022

*To Father...*
(The person who encouraged me in writing
and now lives in my memories)

# Contents


1. THE SCULPTURES ................................. 1

2. IS THEREN'T WAY IN THE EARTH? ........... 53

3. LOVE IN THE LAND ................................. 77

4. WILL THE CAPABILITIES FAIL? .............. 105

# 1.THE SCULPTURES

## DRAMATIS PERSONAE

| | |
|---|---|
| 1. VANAVARAMBAR | - King, Tamil Nadu Kingdom |
| 2. GUNASEELAN | - The sculptor |
| 3. INBAVALLI | - The princess |
| 4. POONGOTHAI | - Inbavalli's friend (Female) |
| 5. RATHINAM | - Gunaseelan's friend (Male) |
| 6. MINISTER | - Minister, Tamil Nadu Kingdom |
| 7. COMMANDER (1) | - Commander, Tamil Nadu Kingdom |
| 8. KANGEYAN | - King, neighbouring Kingdom |
| 9. COMMANDER (2) | - Commander, Kangeyan's Kingdom |
| 10. DOCTOR | - Doctor, Tamil Nadu Kingdom |
| 11. PROCLAIMER | - The Proclaimer, Tamil Nadu |
| 12. PALACE GUARD | - Palace servant, Tamil Nadu Kingdom |
| 13. CIVILIAN – 1 & 2 | - Civilians, Tamil Nadu Kingdom |
| 14. EXECUTIVE OFFICER – 1 & 2 | - Officials, Tamil Nadu |
| 15. SOLDIERS | - Soldiers of Tamil Nadu and Kangeyan Kingdoms |

THE SCULPTURES

## SCENE – 1
**Locale:** The Public Place
**Participants:** The Proclaimer and Two
Civilians

-----------------------------------------------------------------

Drum sound: Dum...Dum...Dum...

*(Beating sound of the drum)*

PROCLAIMER: Cheerful news for the people. The sculpture work going on for two years on the coastal hill of our country is over. The opening ceremony of the sculptures will take place on next Wednesday. King Vanavarambar and Princess Inbavalli will attend the ceremony. Welcome everyone! Welcome!

*(Drum beating Sound)*

CIVILIAN-1: Bro!... Who has carved all these sculptures...?

CIVILIAN-2: Hey Bro... You just asked a good question...All this was carved by our sculptor Gunaseelan. Don't you even know it? The fame would have naturally reached him because of his talent. All right. There's only one week left for the festival. To do awesome decoration all over our street, draw Rangoli at the entrance. We must celebrate it better by erecting the banana trees all the way and tying the buntings from Mango leaf.

CIVILIAN-1: Yes, bro... Let's start work today.


********************************************************************

# SCENE – 2

**Locale:** Chamber of Vanavarambar.
**Participants:** Vanavarambar, Minister and
Guard working at Palace.

------------------------------------------------

PALACE GUARD: Long live the Emperor! whom the
people admire! Majesty, the Minister has come to
meet you.

VANAVARAMBAR: Oh! Is it?... Tell him to come
immediately.

*(The Minister arrives shortly, after the departure of
the palace guard)*

MINISTER: Hello! King ...Greeting homage!

VANAVARAMBAR: Welcome Minister! Come on,
be seated.

*(Minister takes his seat)*

MINISTER: King!... The capital is with a festive
atmosphere like never before in the history. People
are happily seen everywhere and the city is full of
decorations and enthusiastic gabbling. Everyone
is preparing for the 'Sculpture Festival' thinking
and feeling the same, as if their family festival.

VANAVARAMBAR: Well, It's good Minister! How
are  the arrangements done for the ceremony?

MINISTER: The preparatory work for the ceremony
is all over. A golden chariot has been prepared and
to be presented by you to Gunaseelan, the
sculptor, at the ceremony.

# THE SCULPTURES

VANAVARAMBAR: Minister, there is a slight change in the ceremony event. My daughter Inbavalli is good at the art of Dancing, isn't? I think it will be better that her dance debut also be exhibited in conjunction with the ceremony. Besides, I think that it would be appropriate to give a gift to the best sculptor by my daughter, who is the best in dance. What is your opinion?

MINISTER: King!... I hope that your decision with the artistic mind will always be right.

VANAVARAMBAR: Minister... What people are talking about sculptor Gunaseelan?

MINISTER: I can say that no one is surprised there by his talent because, Gunaseelan has already become so popular among the people.

VANAVARAMBAR: Yeah.... Minister, Isn't he the pride of the country?

**************************************************************

## SCENE – 3

**Locale:** Chamber of Inbavalli.
**Participants:** Inbavalli and Poongothai.

---

POONGOTHAI: Princess ... Princess ...

INBAVALLI: Poongothai... What? Why are you coming fast?

POONGOTHAI: Nothing Princess! you have a dance party at the sculpture festival. Haven't you? They have invited you to choose the costumes for it.

INBAVALLI: Oh! Hmmm... I forgot.  One more thing. It is not enough to choose the clothes well rather, the rehearsal should be done properly. I'm scared of being for the first time on the stage, Poongothai!

POONGOTHAI: Don't be afraid of this Princess. Twenty-five-year-old Gunaseelan has carved sculptures which has been admired by the country. Had he been scared, could these things have happened?

INBAVALLI: Do you know him? Have you seen him?

POONGOTHAI: I have not seen but, he is a close friend to my uncle. I know all this, because my uncle told me. Well... it's time to leave.

************************************************************

## SCENE – 4

**Locale:** The Place where the ceremony is scheduled.

**Participants:** Vanavarambar, Inbavalli, Minister, Poongothai, Palace Guard, Gunaseelan, Rathinam and Civilians.

------------------------------------------------------------

PUBLIC:  Long live the king! Long live the king! Long live the Guardian of Art! Long live the Guardian of Art!

VANAVARAMBAR:  Minister... Today is an unforgettable day in my life. On this day of joy, all my imagination has been shaped as sculptures Wow... How people are gathered here like the massive flood? How happy they are!

*(Sound of accordion)*

PALACE GUARD:  The king will open the sculptures now!

*(Vanavarambar pulls a rope and opens the sculptures)*

CIVILIANS: Long live the King! Long live the king!
*(Applause)*

PALACE GUARD:  The princess's dance debut will take place shortly.

*(Princess dances)*
*(Applause)*

********************************************************

# SCENE – 5

**Locale:** Residence of Gunaseelan.

**Participants:** Gunaseelan and Rathinam.

--------------------------------------------------------------

RATHINAM: Gunaseelan... Gunaseelan...

GUNASEELAN: Welcome Rathinam. Come on. Please be seated. Do you eat something?

RATHINAM: I ate a lot to fulfil my stomach. Besides, I have been fulfilled with my niece, Poongothai's speech.

GUNASEELAN: What happened? Did you fight with her?

RATHINAM: Leave it that. Do you know how happy I am to see the people praising you emotionally? Oh! Yes. Why were you watching the dance of princess at the ceremony yesterday without closing your mouth! I was afraid that a fly or a mosquito would enter into your mouth.

GUNASEELAN: *(laughs)* What Rathinam? You're joking. I'm an artist. What's wrong in enjoying a dance performance?

RATHINAM: There is nothing wrong in enjoying the dance performance but, it seems that you have enjoyed it, having lost your heart towards the princess.

GUNASEELAN: You are different. Where am I? Where is she? Why is your imagination going like this?

RATHINAM:  Gunaseela, It seemed to me. So that, I told! That's it! Hmmm... I am going to shop. May I leave?

GUNASEELAN: Ok. Rathinam, Don't forget to come here, when you get free time. While I talk to you, I feel that the time does not seem to pass by so quickly.

RATHINAM:  Gunaseela, What else is there for me to talk to you than anything else? I'll go for the shop and will eat something. That's it! Won't I reach to you at other times?


**************************************************************

## SCENE – 6

**Location:** Chamber of Inbavalli.
**Participants:** Inbavalli and Poongothai.

-------------------------------------------------------------------

POONGOTHAI: The princess seems to be thinking of something important. I think that there is a problem, apart from just her thinking.

INBAVALLI: Poongothai...How can you alone exactly trace my mood? Where did you learn the art of knowing the mind of others?

POONGOTHAI: What's in it? The face is like a mirror showing the mood. If we look at the face, everything is known.

INBAVALLI: Poongothai ... Do you remember saying that your uncle is the friend of the sculptor, Gunaseelan?

POONGOTHAI: Yeah...I had told. What's up with that?

INBAVALLI: Can you help me to visit to the gallery of Gunaseelan, the sculptor? We shall go alone.

POONGOTHAI: *(Cheerfully)* Oh, yes! I understood now that *the cart* is on the track of love. Arranging to meet him is not a big deal. Wouldn't your dad get angry, if he knows?

INBAVALLI: I should go without the knowledge of my father. Can you please arrange?

POONGOTHAI: Hmm... *The cart made of love* is fast. You have said so much. Leave the fear. Somehow, I will help you to meet him.

# THE SCULPTURES

## SCENE – 7

**Location:** Chamber of Vanavarambar.

**Participants:** Vanavarambar and Minister.

------------------------------------------------------------

VANAVARAMBAR: Come on Minister. What sort of steps have you taken to maintain the sculptures? Have any you done special arrangements?

MINISTER: Oh! King, I just came to report it and leave. A maintenance team consisting of fifty members has been set up. It is also arranged to grow flowering plants around the hills. King! There is another happy news. The popularity of sculptures has spread even to the neighbouring countries. Many kings have sent the letters to visit our country to visit the sculptures.

VANAVARAMBAR: Really?... My wish is that the pride of our country should spread all the globe. The time for the same is nearing. Minister! Hmm...Make sure to do all the arrangements to treat the visiting kings and anyone shouldn't criticize the hospitality of our country.

**************************************************************

## SCENE – 8

**Locale:** Residence of Gunaseelan.

**Participants:** Gunaseelan and Rathinam.

----------------------------------------------------------------

RATHINAM: What Gunaseelan?... Is all the work done?

GUNASEELAN: Come on Rathinam. Is there any special news? You are often worried about your niece Poongothai, referring her as chatterer! Has she kept her mouth shut? or Are you subdued her?

RATHINAM: Why are you asking about it? Can the mouth easily be subdued? She is a friend of the Princess. Do we want to ask that? She is so garrulous. I have come to a conclusion that we need to keep a target date. If she doesn't subdue within that, I would become a monk. How is my decision?

GUNASEELAN: *(Laughs)* It seems that you're in agony but, don't give up the effort. The reason is that the so-called literature says that women are soft.

RATHINAM: Hey!... Damn it. Those poets who sang about women meekness and they should be allowed to talk to Poongothai for a day. They will then know that everything that they have written is wrong. They will run away pleading us to leave them. Damn...Did you see? I keep telling my story. I forgot the message that I wanted to inform. The Princess want to see your the sculpture gallery. In this regard, the Princess and Poongothai would visit here on a single day. I came to say that first but I was discussing the other things.

GUNASEELAN:  What is the need to visit like that alone? Didn't you ask the reason?

RATHINAM:  Who knows? I can say that the reason is due to exchange of eyes that happened at the festival.

GUNASEELAN:  Don't play Rathinam. I really don't understand the reason for the arrival of the Princess!

RATHINAM:  Haven't you understood? Sleep calmly today. You will understand everything tomorrow.


*****************************************************************

## SCENE – 9

**Location:** Chamber of Vanavarambar.

**Participants:** Vanavarambar and Inbavalli.

------------------------------------------------------------

INBAVALLI: Dad... Did you call me?

VANAVARAMBAR: Come on daughter! I was just thinking about you. Remember what I told you earlier. Hmm... I'm talking about your wedding. There are letters obtained from many kings to select you as life partner. I am waiting for your decision daughter!

INBAVALLI: What is the hurry for my wedding in the meantime, dad? There are many more domains left in the Art of Dance to get experienced and I also desire to gain knowledge in multidisciplinary fields. After that, I shall tell you about marriage, Dad!

VANAVARAMBAR: Daughter... Your marriage has to be completed soon. couldn't I have that desire of conducting your marriage? Tell me yourself!

INBAVALLI: Dad...do you think that I should leave our country, soon after marriage?

VANAVARAMBAR: What are you talking dear? Don't you know how much misery it is for me to be separated from you whom I nurtured like my eyes? Saplings sprout under the banana tree, but leaving them it will be of useless. Only when it is transplanted and planted somewhere else, it grows and bears good fruits. Girls are also like that daughter! Their life is complete only, when they are separated from their place of birth and live in the arms of a man. That's what, I came to say. You have made my eyes to wet, daughter!

INBAVALLI: Dad, I didn't say no to marriage. I just asked, why should I prepare myself for it in such a hurry?

VANAVARAMBAR: Okay daughter. Don't rush for it. I will give you all the letters where they have demanded you as bride. You shall choose one your favourites from those kings. Tell me your decision, as soon as possible.

************************************************************

## SCENE –10

**Location:** Residence of Gunaseelan.
**Participants:** Gunaseelan, Rathinam,
Inbavalli and Poongothai.

---

RATHINAM: Favoured... favoured... good luck has favoured us.

GUNASEELAN: What do you mean by that Rathinam? What happened?

RATHINAM: The goddess who desires to give something will tear the roof and give. *(*Native Proverb)*. That's what I came to say...

GUNASEELAN: Don't talk around, Rathinam... Tell me what's the matter?

RATHINAM: The matter is..! The princess would arrive here in a short while for witnessing your sculptures. It is not only to visit the sculptures, but also to meet you.

*(At this time Invavalli and Poonkothai arrive at a short distance from Gunaseelan's place)*

RATHINAM: Damn... Gunaseela... The Princess has come. *(In a mild voice)* Go... go!.... welcome and get them inside! Don't stand idle! It's a royal matter.

*(Gunaseelan welcomes the princess)*

# THE SCULPTURES

GUNASEELAN:  Come on princess... come on! I am proud that you visited this simple sculptor's gallery. Please be seated...Can I bring something to drink?

INBAVALLI:  No ...Don't do all that. I just came to see you. *(With a lowered voice)* Hmmm... I mean, I came here to witness your sculptures and leave. *(To Poongothai)* Isn't, Poongothai?

POONGOTHAI:  Yeah...Yeah...Gunaseelan... Ma'am has the desire. Do you wish to ask what sort of desire? Just to see your sculptures. That's why, I alone accompanied with her!

INBAVALLI:  Yeah...Yeah... you're right. *(Pointing to the Rathinam)* Who is this? Is he your friend?

RATHINAM:  Greetings...I thought of introducing myself first but, when an elder speaks, interfering in their speech becomes overacting. That's why, I didn't address. Let's say, *The fibre that is attached to the flower also smells* *(Native Proverb)*. Just like that, Gunaseelan is like a flower... I'm like a fibre... I am Rathinam... This is my history!

INBAVALLI:  *(Laughs)* Poongothai... Is he the person whom you told?

POONGOTHAI:  Oh Princess! I am blushed, as you ask me directly face to face.

RATHINAM: Princess...Let me tell you. Don't have doubts. She is my wonderful niece. She might have told you everything... *(to Poongothai)* Poongothai... Did you tell our concern to Princess?

*(Inbavalli Laughs)*

POONGOTHAI: Oops... you don't talk. Princess, you go and look at the sculptures and return. I am here.

RATHINAM:  Gunaseelan... Lead the Princess... I'll be right here too.

GUNASEELAN:  Come on Princess. Let's go into the sculpture gallery.

*(Inbavalli and Gunaseelan enter the sculpture gallery)*

**************************************************************

# THE SCULPTURES

## SCENE – 11
**Locale:** The sculpture gallery.
**Participants:** Gunaseelan and Inbavalli.

---------------------------------------------------------

GUNASEELAN:    Princess... This is the first sculpture that I carved.

INBAVALLI: Is it? How realistically you have shaped the connection between mother and child? Hmm...May I know where your mother and father are?

GUNASEELAN:  My mother and father may had died, when I was three years old. I had no idea how I grew up. I had been eating with an assistance of my grandmother, since the day I knew the details.

INBAVALLI:  I think that I have hurt your feeling, asking your mother and father.

GUNASEELAN:  There is no such thing. You asked just to know that! Hmm... Next, this sculpture represents the primitive man.

INBAVALLI:  Oh...it can be seen that the primitive man wandered like an animal with animal...The next sculpture is about the *Art of Stick-Fighting* (*'Silambattam' in Tamil*). Am I right?

GUNASEELAN: Yeah!... The art which excels among all the sports in the world is our native *Stick-Fighting*. That's why, I had carved it.

INBAVALLI:    Next    sculpture    refers    to *Bharatanatyam*. It looks like witnessing the rapid dance performance of two women...Do you know *The Art of Dancing?*

GUNASEELAN:  I am not familiar with the dance, but have the inclination towards *Bharatanatyam.* I sculptured it as an expression of that. I have heard that you are also a Master in Dance. Your performance was very spectacular at that function.

INBAVALLI:  My thanks is for your compliment and I have a request to you. Will you accept it?

GUNASEELAN:  Say what. I consider it as my duty to fulfil the same.

INBAVALLI:  I am younger than you and you should call me by name. Would you do?

GUNASEELAN:  Princess ... you are saying... *(stumbles)*

*(Poongothai comes in from outside)*

POONGOTHAI: Princess ... Princess ... Time runs out. We must be in the palace at the specified time. Shall we depart?

INBAVALLI:  *(To Gunaseelan)* Hmm... I'm going. You just don't forget my request.

*************************************************************

## SCENE – 12
**Locale:** Residence of Gunaseelan.
**Participants:** Gunaseelan and Rathinam.

---

RATHINAM: Gunaseelan... Why do you look different as heartbroken or thoughtful? Tell me, whatever it is. Let me see, whether I can fix it or not!

GUNASEELAN: Nothing Rathinam. I'm just thinking about the princess who arrived and left last day.

RATHINAM: Hey!... I told you on that day, but you denied stating this or that... Now, do you see *'the cat coming out of the bag'*?

GUNASEELAN: Rathinam! I'm in the same state till now, but I am amazed thinking how the human mind frequently changes.

RATHINAM: I mean, now your mind has changed and that's all you have to say... is it?

GUNASEELAN: No... I'm just thinking about the Princess' mind right now.

RATHINAM: Why do you doubt about it? Unless she desires you, will she come alone to visit the sculpture gallery? Will she ever tell you that you should call her by name? Hmm...No matter how, you're very lucky...

GUNASEELAN: Rathinam... You are singing the same refrain. I am thinking about the future.

RATHINAM:   Gunaseelan...Why are you beating around bush? Will you tell without hiding, what's in your mind? Do you have a desire towards the Princess or not?...

GUNASEELAN:  Rathinam...What I want to say is...

RATHINAM:   You do not need to come here either to say anything or go anywhere. Whether you say 'yes' or 'no', whatever is determined to happen, would happen...I am happy to remember the pride that will embark on you. You are worried about something...Okay... It is time. May I leave? Let's meet tomorrow...

***********************************************************

## **SCENE – 13**

**Locale:** Residence of Gunaseelan.
**Participants:** Gunaseelan and Inbavalli.

------------------------------------------------------------

*(Inbavalli arrives alone at Gunaseelan's sculpture gallery in the early morning)*

GUNASEELAN:  Princess...You're alone here in this morning... I would have come to the palace myself, if you had invited!

INBAVALLI:  I had a miraculous dream yesterday. Happy dream too! That's why, I visited here to tell you the same.

GUNASEELAN:  Why should you tell your dream to me?

INBAVALLI:  You are also involved in that dream... In that dream, you are carving a beautiful sculpture. A woman nearby is assisting you. You are tirelessly able to continue and complete the carving work. The sculpture turns into a very beautiful shape. This is my dream.

GUNASEELAN:  You came here a few days ago. Didn't you? You might have fallen asleep with the memory of the sculptures. That is why, sculpture has travelled in your dreams.

INBAVALLI:  You never asked about the girl was who was assisting you in that dream!

GUNASEELAN: Oh!... Who's that? I don't have any lady usurper with me?

INBAVALLI: It's none other than me, the girl who appeared in that dream!

GUNASEELAN: Princess....!

INBAVALLI: Why wouldn't you accept me as your *Page*? Don't I have that qualification?

GUNASEELAN: Princess...you know yourself that your dream is an impossible fantasy to happen.

INBAVALLI: Making that dream come true is in your hands or my life will end in a dream itself.

GUNASEELAN: Princess... there is a history of adding milk and water. Can water and oil be added together? Answer yourself.

INBAVALLI: Don't think of separating and brushing aside me. Don't create a situation where I set aside this world.

GUNASEELAN: Princess ... What do you say?

INBAVALLI: Don't call me Princess. In a few more days, you will know what my condition is, unless you realize that my life is devoted to you.

GUNASEELAN: Inbavalli!

INBAVALLI: Dear... you at least just thought of calling me by name!

GUNASEELAN: You changed my mind and made it yours! I grew up poor, but I have never been a coward. I testify over the Sun that no force in this world can separate the two of us.

24

**********************************************************

## SCENE – 14

**Locale:** Chamber of Vanavarambar.
**Participants:** Vanavarambar and Minister.

-----------------------------------------------

MINISTER: King... an important message! I hurried, because the news is about the Princess.

VANAVARAMBAR: Yeah! ... come on Minister. Is the news about Inbavalli? or her marriage?

MINISTER: No king! Every day, our princess secretly goes to the sculptor's gallery of the sculptor, Gunaseelan. Having noticed the same for few days, one of our spies told that she solely departed from the palace, visited that gallery and returned.

VANAVARAMBAR: Minister! Why has Inbavalli gone to Gunaseelan's sculpture gallery? I don't understand anything! I would like to know immediately whether this news is true or false.

MINISTER: King! Has the Princess fallen in love with Gunaseelan?

VANAVARAMBAR: Oh...minister...what are you saying? Is my daughter in love with Gunaseelan? It can never be! How can the king's daughter fall in love with after all with a sculptor! Hmm...Who is there?

PALACE GUARD: Yes Lord! ... my king...

VANAVARAMBAR: Tell the Princess to meet me right away!

## **SCENE – 15**

**Locale:** Chamber of Vanavarambar.
**Participants:** Vanavarambar, Inbavalli and Palace Guard.

---

INBAVALLI: Dad...I knew you called in a hurry. Any important news dad?

VANAVARAMBAR:  Inbavalli... Is what I heard true...?

INBAVALLI: What do I answer, if asked whether it is true without saying what it is. I think you are angry.

VANAVARAMBAR: Do you go to meet the sculptor Gunaseelan every day, that too in secret? I ask you whether this is true.

INBAVALLI: Dad... everything you heard is true.

VANAVARAMBAR: Daughter...Why did you go there? I don't even know that!

INBAVALLI: Dad...You are the one who raised me being as mother and father. Will I say it someone without telling you the truth? My mind went along with him, when I presented the gift to Gunaseela at the ceremony on that day. Whenever you asked about my marriage, I was late because I was reluctant to tell you this news. Forgive me for not telling you about this in the beginning, dad!

VANAVARAMBAR: Shame! Shame on you! daughter. The value of the royal family has been destroyed! You are saying that you have lost your mind towards that sculptor who fits for nothing,

while plethora of kings is marching to marry you! How did you prepare your mind to commit this filthy act, daughter?

INBAVALLI:  Dad, please don't hurt my mind! Tell me, don't I have the right to choose the one who deserves my life.

VANAVARAMBAR: Yeah...daughter! You have the right, but you just think about whom you have chosen.

INBAVALLI: I loved a good man, Dad! I have chosen someone who excels the best in all virtues and art.

VANAVARAMBAN: Inbavalli...It is natural for the mind to be restless like this in young age, but you shouldn't imagine something that doesn't ever happen and should not ever to happen. You forget him completely. I will soon make you to marry one of your favourite kings who wrote a letter asking to be bride. Is it right?

INBAVALLI: Dad, if I forget and marry someone else, it is like losing my eyes and buying a picture... Please do not force me, dad!

VANAVARAMBAN:  Inbavalli...you know my character very well! I will never allow this act which loses our dignity. Daughter, listen to what your father says! Change your mind in a right away.

INBAVALLI: You can tell me to lose my life, but don't just tell me to change my mind! I can't do that!

VANAVARAMBAR: Hm... *Really?*... Look what I am doing to Gunaseelan who gave you this much courage. Who is there?

INBAVALLI: Dad... Don't do anything to him. He is ignorant of any sin. Just listen to what I say.

*(The Palace Guard comes)*

PALACE GUARD: Greetings... King!

VANAVARAMBAR: Bring the unscrupulous sculptor, Gunaseelan to the palace immediately! He came to destroy the pride of the royal family,

PALACE GUARD: Order, O' king!

*(The Palace Guard goes. The king quickly goes inside. Inbavalli stands with bursting into tears in eyes)*

**************************************************************

## SCENE – 16

**Locale:** Residence of Gunaseelan.
**Participants:** Gunaseelan, Rathinam and
Palace Guard.

---

RATHINAM: Gunaseela...Do you know the thing? Just now Poongothai ran out of the palace and told me that the king has been informed about your love affair. The king has ordered you to be brought to the palace immediately. You just escape from here and go somewhere. Don't get caught into problem...Do you understand?  Hmm ... Leave immediately.

GUNASEELAN:  Don't be panic Rathinam. This is exactly what I expected before. Inbavalli had already told me that I should talk to the king about our marriage. Now, that the king has summoned me. Therefore, I have less difficulty. That's it! I can't go anywhere else from here for this. I am not a coward to live in hiding. Tell me, will fleeing away in fear solve the problem?

RATHINAM:  What Gunaseelan, you talk like this! I think that you still don't understand the peril that will embark on you. First, you need to get out of here. Later, we shall patiently see the things that are yet to happen.

GUNASEELAN:  Rathinam... I can't move even one foot away from my location. I am going to the king and tell him my opinion. In pursuit, whatever is to happen, let it happen.

*(Footsteps is heard from the doorway. A Palace Guard arrives shortly after)*

THE SCULPTURES

PALACE GUARD: Gunaseelan...I have come to take you to the king.

GUNASEELAN: *(to the Palace Guard)* Hmm...Let's leave! *(to Rathinam)* Rathinam... Take care of the house, until I return here. I will be back soon. What...? Do you understand?

RATHINAM: Okay... leave for now and return for sure! There will no danger for your pure mind.

*(Gunaseelan leaves with the Palace Guard)*

****************************************************************

## SCENE – 17

**Locale:** Chamber of King's Council.

**Participants:** Vanavarambar, Minister, Inbavalli, Gunaseelan, Soldiers and Visitors.

-------------------------------------------------------------------

VANAVARAMBAR: Gunaseela... Do you know what a big mistake have you committed?

GUNASEELAN: Oh Majesty! May I know the mistake, as you said, to have been committed by me?

VANAVARAMBAR: Don't you know that it is wrong for an ordinary sculptor to fall in love with a Princess? After committing a mistake, you are asking me a question that too differently.

GUNASEELN: Oh King!... Don't you know? I am a sculptor, but I too have the heart and the same has also feeling in it. My involvement with the princess is not in anticipation of gold or material, rather only on the basis of love. You define love, as to love someone who deserves the same with status. In what way, is it fair to restrict the union of love between a man and a woman? My majesty! Answer graciously.

VANAVARAMBAR: Gunaseelan... I thought that you were talented in sculpture making, but I just realize that you are also good at talking. As a King I command, change your mind immediately. Forget her right away, if you have a desire for life.

GUNASEELAN:  My majesty!... If you say so, to whom should I appeal? Don't divide us by heart. Don't restrain our love. I swear by the art I have

learned that I can't even imagine life without Inbavalli, O' majesty!

VANAVARAMBAR: Gunaseelan... I understand you! I learned from your speech that you can never change. Minister...Take this stubborn man to the dungeon. Keep him away from sight. Give him a chance one day, till tomorrow. If he does not change his mind, banish him the next day. This is my order!

INBAVALLI: *(comes suddenly)* Dad...What a horrible thing! This sentence is for the one who does no harm! If punishment is for the love, then, I am the reason for his love. Punish me too.

VANAVARAMBAR: Inbavalli...Why did you come here? Hmm...Who is there? Take her to her room! Minister... Execute my order exactly.

*(Attendees forcibly take Inbavalli inside.)*

****************************************************************

## SCENE – 18

**Locale:** Chamber of Vanavarambar.
**Participants:** Vanavarambar, Minister and
Commander (1)

---

*(Minister and Commander are coming fast)*

VANAVARAMBAR:   Come on... Why are the Minister and the Commander coming at the same time, that too with tension?

MINISTER:  O' king... Danger. Great danger to our country.

VANAVARAMBAR:  Minister...  what  are  you saying? Is there a danger?

MINISTER:   My majesty... King Kangeyan of the neighbouring country has been invading towards our country in a single night. The spy has sent word that his forces may besiege our fort by tomorrow morning.

COMMANDER -1:  Half of our troops have already gone many miles for training and don't know how to deal with the invasion at this time.

VANAVARAMBAR: Why did the Kangeyan invade our country? There is no enmity between him and us! Minister... Didn't a single spy at least get any news about the purpose of the invasion?

MINISTER:  I don't know anything about that, King! But it is clearly known that he had departed from his country.

VANAVARAMBAR:     Commander...Prepare our army! What is the purpose of the deceiver? We must resist with determination at any cost. Immediately inform the soldiers to be ready for battle. Hurry up...

*(Minister and Commander depart. King stands reflecting with deep thoughts inside)*

**************************************************************

## SCENE – 19

*(A fierce battle ensues between the Tamil Nadu forces and the Kangeyan army. Eventually, the Kangeyan army defeats and enters into the fort.)*

**************************************************************

## **SCENE – 20**

**Locale:** Chamber of King's Council.
**Participants:** Vanavarambar, Minister,
Kangeyan and Commander (2).

------------------------------------------------------------

KANGEYAN: Ha... ha...! Oh Vanavarambar...!
I appreciate your heroism, but I just got the victory
towards the end.

VANAVARAMBAR: Kangeya...What was the
purpose of your sudden invasion? Didn't you know
that waging war without warning is a cowardly
act? Understand that this is not a victory for you!

KANGEYAN: Ha... ha...! Oh Vanavarambar...!
Everything you say is correct, but my goal is
important for me. I don't think about all the means
to achieve it.

VANAVARAMBAR: Kangeyan...What is your
purpose?

KANGEYAN: Ask like that! Your country's fame
seems to be spread all over the world. My purpose
is to prevent that.

VANAVARAMBAR: I don't understand your
speech. Tell clearly regarding the reason for your
invasion!

KANGEYAN: Let me explain. Don't you know that
the fame of your country's sculptures spreads

across the world? or do you pretend as if you don't to know? I also know that many kings have come

here to visit the sculptures. I don't think that it is right for your country to be more famous, than my country. My forces have entered your castle to prevent your fame from spreading! Do you understand my purpose now?

VANAVARAMBAR: Our country has always been the best in art. Kangeyan, you can't destroy even an iota of the reputation of our country.

KANGEYAN:  See that if I can destroy it or not! Commander... Depart with our troops to the place where the sculptures are kept. Destroy the sculptures with the powerful weapons that we have brought. Not even a single sculpture should exist there; rather stones alone should be there. When it is completed, we must return to our country by this evening.

VANAVARAMBAR:  Kangeyan...What a heinous act is this? Are you going to demolish the sculptures? Do not do it just like that. Those sculptures are like my life! I can't bear to see them destroyed. Kangeyan, I beg you. I will give you as much material, as you want. Don't just destroy only those art icons!

KANGEYAN:  Material is not important to me. Vanavarambar, your country should never have the reputation which my country does not have. Those sculptures should never be! Hmmm... Commander, leave immediately.


************************************************************

## **SCENE – 21**
### *(Soldiers destroy the sculptures)*

***************************************************************

## **SCENE – 22**
**Locale:** Chamber of King's Council.
**Participants:** Kangeyan, Commander (2), Vanavarambar and Gunaseelan.

------------------------------------------------------------------

*(Kangeyan's commander brings Gunaseelan)*

COMMANDER – 2: O' King... we have destroyed all the sculptures. They have been smashed and are beyond recognition.

KANGEYAN: Well, done! *(Pointing at Gunaseelan)* Who is he? Why did you bring him here?

COMMANDER – 2: Majesty... His name is Gunaseelan, an excellent sculptor. He was kept in a dungeon. He is very obstinate. He refuses to speak. We asked by intimidating others and it is revealed that it was he who carved out all those glorious sculptures. He has fallen in love with the king's daughter. Therefore, he confined him in jail!

KANGEYAN: Ha... ha... is there such a thing? Well...let's go of his handcuffs. We have to take him to our country as well. Hmm... let's go! Vanavarambar...The work that I came here is over. Bye.

***************************************************************

## SCENE – 23

**Locale:** Chamber of Vanavarambar.

**Participants:** Vanavarambar and Minister.

---

VANAVARAMBAR: Minister... Alas! He has destroyed all my art treasures!... I have protected them like my eyes! I would have given my life in return! What am I going to do now?

MINISTER: King... the people are confused by this sudden invasion. The first thing is to make them to be at peace. If you find yourself discouraged, what can we all do?

VANAVARAMBAR: Minister...I could not bear this loss. Ah!... my heart aches! My arms and legs are trembling, Minister...

*(King's body is trembling)*

MINISTER: Ah!... my King... just sit there. I call the doctor right away. I think that your body is fatigue due to the shock.

*(The minister leaves the king from bed and goes fast to call the doctor)*

***************************************************************

## SCENE – 24

**Locale:** Chamber of Vanavarambar.
**Participants:** Vanavarambar, Minister and
Doctor.

----------------------------------------------------------------

*(The Doctor examines the King and then, speaks to
the Minister)*

MINISTER:  Doctor...How is the king's health? Is he
normal?

DOCTOR:  No Minister...He has rheumatism due to
shock. I can't say, when it will get healed! However,
I have given the very best herbal medicine. See you
tomorrow.

*(As soon as the doctor leaves, the minister comes
near the king's bed).*

VANAVARAMBAR: Oh! Minister... What did the
doctor say about my health?

MINISTER:  He has stated that your health will
improve soon. Shall I order to bring some food for
you now?

VANAVARAMBAR: Nothing is required, Minister...
I couldn't even move with my legs! I think that my
health will not improve anymore!

MINISTER: My King...I'm very hopeful that you will
get well soon and I beseech you to take rest.

VANAVARAMBAR: How is my daughter Inbavalli?
I have not seen her for two days!

MINISTER: The actions of the Princess have greatly changed. O' king! She is seen with a frowning face and tears in her eyes, since she learns that Gunaseelan has been taken away by Kangeyan. I offered her the words of comfort. Yet, she did not change her mind.

VANAVARAMBAR: Daughter, Oh! My precious daughter. Is it you who has to endure this tragic condition? Minister... do not reveal my health condition to her. Insist her friends to to assist her to resume towards normalcy. It has become a reality: *"The misfortunes never come single."*

MINISTER: My King! you take rest. Everything will go well.

VANAVARAMBAR: Well, Minister... Please comfort my daughter, somehow!

*************************************************************

## **SCENE – 25**

**Locale:** Public Space.
**Participants:** Two civilians.

---

CIVILIAN – 1: Bro... Do you witness the restless situation in our country? 'What will happen next and next' is the situation that has been felt by everyone for the last one month here!

CIVILIAN - 2: Yes bro.! When the king imprisoned the innocent brother Gunaseelan who had committed nothing wrong, the worst time had started to our country. Did you witness that Kangeyan invaded the country on the next day itself and destroyed all the sculptures?

CIVILIAN - 1: That's right brother...but, can Gunaseelan fall in love with the Princess? That is why, the king imprisoned him...

CIVILIAN – 2: Hey! bro... You speak, as if the king's action is right. While the Princess wholeheartedly loves the sculptor, shall we see the difference like sculptor and a princess? Do you know that magnum opus Tamil text like *Thirukural* proclaims the greatness of love? The king who has read everything shouldn't have punished our Gunaseelan, all of a sudden!

CIVILIAN - 1: You are right bro...! Then...it seems that Kangeyan has captured Gunaseelan too!

CIVILIAN - 2: That's why, I'm worried about that. Our sculptor doesn't even harm either a fly or a crow. I don't know what is that scoundrel going to do him?

CIVILIAN - 1: The king is also not in good health. All are gossiping that the Princess has also changed to melancholic state and become idiosyncratic, after the separation from Gunaseelan... Tell me, is this true...?

CIVILIAN - 2: Yeah...bro. I heard the same thing. At this stage, the country witnesses the revolt and fight here and there. When will the chaos of our country be resolved? When will the good fortune reach us?

***************************************************************

## **SCENE – 26**

**Locale:** Chamber of Minister.
**Participants:** Minister and Commander – 1.

-------------------------------------------------------------------

MINISTER:  Come on Commander... I was waiting for you.

COMMANDER – 1:  Hello Minister... Is there any urgent news?

MINISTER:  Commander... very, very urgent news. The problems in the country are developing day by day. These must be placed to an end. Now, it is necessary to know exactly the situation prevailing in different parts of the country. For that, the Executive Council of our country should be convened immediately. What is your opinion?

COMMANDER – 1:  Minister...I agree with your opinion. Knowing that the king is sick, evil spirits began to appear in some places. Riots have been initiated. Stringent action must be taken before the same spreading across the country.

MINISTER:  That is why, I say Commander that we will convene the Executive Council of the country immediately. Let's inform to all the authorities. The executive council should be convened within two days.

COMMANDER – 1: What you are saying is the right idea. I am sending a message to all executives today.

*****************************************************************

## SCENE – 27

**Locale:** Chamber of King's Council.
**Participants:** Minister, Commander – 1, Executive Officer - 1, Executive Officer – 2 and Gunaseelan.

-----------------------------------------------------------------

*(Board of Executive is convened)*

MINISTER: Hello...! Executive Officers... The Board of Executives has been hurriedly convened to discuss the present situation in our country and then the steps to be taken in future. I have received the reports that riots have broken out in some parts of the country and there has been turbulence among the people. I would like to know from you that whether those messages are true or not.

EXECUTIVE OFFICER - 1: Commander! I adore you. The insurgency in the Northeast province is under my administration and growing uncontrollably. Rumours are often spread about the palace, it also causes the riots. Two lives were lost in the riots that erupted yesterday.

MINISTER: Really?... Is the Northeast province being like this?... Hmm... Ok. Next, how is the situation in your West province?

EXECUTIVE OFFICER - 2: Minister... In my area, some hooligans have been involved in robberies at unexpected times for the past one week. The robbery could not be controlled, even though the soldiers were deployed for custody. They came with mask and looted. Hence, people couldn't identify who they were. This had caused panic among the people. Normal life is affected!

MINISTER: Commander...! Is it possible to know that the civil riot is increasing through the information received form the officials? How shall it be controlled? Do you have any idea?

COMMANDER-1: Minister...in my opinion, the root cause of everything is that the king is bedridden. Someone must temporarily sworn in for the country, until the king recovers and resumes to his normalcy.

MINISTER: Commander...What you are saying? Is it a good idea? but the challenging task is that who will be chosen for it!

COMMANDER-1: Minister...I have an idea. What if the princess shall temporarily be asked to sworn in? Doing so, no one shall blame. I think that the problems will also be solved as well.

MINISTER: That's a good idea too. Will the Princess agree to this? She has completely changed, since Gunaseelan had left! It is not known that can a Princess who doesn't speak properly to anyone and does not eat properly due to the tragedy take the responsibility?

*(At this time, the Minister witnesses someone staggering at the door of Courtyard).*

COMMANDER-1: Ah...! Minister... Look at that. Someone is staggering at the door. Tell them to hold him on right away. Make him to be seated.

*(Bustle continues in the crowd. The commander visits near the person who has come. He recognizes that it is Gunaseelan).*

Minister... this is none other than our sculptor Gunaseelan!

MINISTER: Opps!... Gunaseelan? It seems that the hair and beard have drastically grown up and he is totally unidentified! He seems to be very weird. *(To the guards)* Immediately offer him fruit juice. Take him to a private room and rest him on the bed. Hmm... Commander...We can gather the information from Gunaseelan tomorrow and have the discussion later. Yes...Ladies and gentlemen... With this, the House dissolves.

************************************************************

## **SCENE – 28**

**Locale:** Palace Room.

**Participants:** Minister and Gunaseelan.

------------------------------------------------------------

*(Gunaseelan gets up and sits on the bed, after the slumber)*

MINISTER: Gunaseelan... Is your health Okay? Do you know the place where you are?

GUNASEELAN: Minister... I am in our country. I am at my motherland only.

MINISTER: Yeah! Gunaseelan... You are in the palace of our country! You came here yesterday in the unconscious state. You woke up well this morning!

GUNASEELAN: Dear Minister... Has Kangeyan destroyed all the sculptures of our country? Is it true that he demolished all the sculptures, which were created by day and night for two years?

MINISTER: Yeah! Gunaseelan... It is generally stated that many days are needed for those who strive and one day is enough for those who plunder. It just happened so. It was on the day when the sculptures were destroyed, the king had fallen sick from that day onwards. The health has not healed yet. The king's physical condition has been very bad for the last two days. The princess has not been in stable, since you left the country. Our country is tottering like a small boat stuck in the ocean.

GUNASEELAN: Minister... I must see the king immediately. Can you arrange?

MINISTER:  Come on!  Let's go see the king right
    now.


************************************************************

## **SCENE – 29**

**Locale:** Chamber of Vanavarambar.
**Participants:** Vanavarambar, Minister, Gunaseelan, Inbavalli and Maids.

------------------------------------------------------------

*(The king lays on the bed)*

MINISTER: *(Slowly)* My King!... Look here! Our sculptor Gunaseelan has arrived.

GUNASEELAN:  Hello...King!

*(King turns slowly)*

VANAVARAMBAR:        *(in      a      mild      voice)* Ah...Gunaseelan... come on!  When did you come? Did Kangeyan free you? *(with astonishment)*

GUNASEELAN:   No majesty!... I myself escaped from him and reached here. On the way of the journey, he sojourned in a place, having erected a tent. During that time that is after reaching his country, he insisted me that that I should devise and offer the sculptures there, as it was already carved in our country. I refuted him saying: "You have destroyed the artistic wealth of my motherland so; I can never do what you have asked me to do". Therefore, soon after reaching his country, I felt that either he would force me to carve the sculptures or if I refuse, he will persecute me.

Everyone was asleep at that night. Unnoticed by others, I fled from the backside of the tent in the middle of the night. As I knew neither the direction nor way, I stayed in the forest, mountains and hideouts for a month and eventually reached our country last day only.

VANAVARAMBAR: Gunaseelan... how confident you are! How patriotic are you for our motherland? While I think about you, it fills my heart. Alas! I had unnecessarily punished you...

GUNASEELAN: Oh! my king...Don't worry about the sculptures being destroyed. I can carve the sculptures even better than before. I can create those art forms very soon King! The fame of our country's flag is going to sway all over the world again.

VANAVARAMBAR: You poured milk in my stomach Gunaseelan...Every atom of my body now greets you. Hmm...Minister...How is Inbavalli? Tell them to bring her to me.

*(Maids bring Inbavalli)*

MINISTER: Here, the princess herself is on the way, my King!

*(Inbavalli comes near the king's bed bowing her head)*

VANAVARAMBAR: Daughter... did you see that our sculptor Gunaseelan has arrived?

*(Inbavalli straightens and looks at Gunaseelan)*

INBAVALLI: *(in a troubled voice)* Ah!... my dear... Have you come?... Isn't there any danger to you?

GUNASEELAN: Inbavalli, Why are your eyes troubled? I have no suffering.

VANAVARAMBAR:  Daughter... Inbavalli... Come here!

INBAVALLI: Dad...

*(Inbavalli sits on the bed where Vanavarambar lays)*

VANAVARAMBAR:  Don't worry daughter...The time has come for all your thoughts to become true. Hmm... Gunaseelan... you too come near me!

GUNASEELAN: King...

*(King holds Inbavalli's hand and joints it with Gunaseelan's hand)*

VANAVARAMBAR: Gunaseelan... I entrust to you my dear daughter and this precious country. From now onwards, you have to protect my daughter and the country. My heartfelt congratulation is to both of you!

*(King leaves his last breath)*

MINISTER AND GUNASEELAN:  Alas!... King!...

INBAVALLI:  Alas!.... Dad...!

**(The End)**

**********************************************************

# 2. IS THEREN'T WAY IN THE EARTH?

## DRAMATIS PERSONAE

1. RAJA          - Unemployed youth.

2. BABU         - Raja's Friend.

3. CHELLAPPA   - Raja's College mate.

4. NALLASIVAM - Businessman.

5. MANAGER    - Office Manager, Raja is going to attend an interview with him.

6. MANI         - One who accompanies with Raja for an interview.

7. PEON         - He works as Peon at the office where Raja goes for interview.

8. MADAM       - Leady Head.

*******************************************************

## **SCENE – 1**
**Locale:** In front of the Office.
**Participants:** Raja, Mani, Peon and two others.

*(Raja is seated with file and two more others are seated along with him. Mani is seated having snake gourd and a bag in his hands.)*

-------------------------------------------------------------

PEON: Who is Mani here?

*(Everyone looks at each other without exchanging any   word.)*

GUYS. . . who is Mani among you?

*(As suddenly got a flash in his mind, Mani fixes an ear hearing aid in his ear)*

Hasn't anybody come here as Mani?

MANI: *(Stood up hastily)* and proclaimed "I am Mani. I am Mani".

PEON: Hey, chap… Are you? I am shrieking wildly. You are lethargically seated.

MANI: Sorry sir.

PEON: Ok.. Ok…Manager calls you… get in.

*(Mani goes inside the chamber of Manager. Unfortunately, his ear aid has fallen.*

See! How has he come to an interview?

*(Looking at the paper in his hand)*

Hmmm.... Next... who is Raja?

RAJA   : I am the one.

PEON   : Next person will be "you", be ready...

*****************************************************

## SCENE - 2
**Locale:** Office
**Participants:** Manager and Mani.

*(Mani enters having a bag in his hand and a snake gourd on his shoulder)*

--------------------------------------------------------------

MANAGER: Who is that? What do you want?

*(Having been seated on the chair, Mani shows an offer letter, not uttering a single word.)*

Oh! Have you come for an interview? What is your good name?

MANI: I have completed B.Com sir!

MANAGER: I asked your name.

MANI: Is it my age sir? I am 25.

MANAGER: *(in a mild voice)* what? Couldn't he lend his ears? . . . He gives wrong answers for all the raised questions.

*(Manager closely observes him. His ear aid machine is hanging, without being attached to his ears).*

Oh! I could understand your problem.

*(He shows the gesture towards Mani conveying a message that he needs to attach his ear aid machine).*

MANI: Thank you sir, I will answer without having it.

MANAGER: Ya...ya.. I could see it for a while...Then...what are all these?... Bag and snake gourd...what Mr.?

MANI: Sorry sir. As I started to market to get some provisions and veggies, ... I came here with the thought to attend the interview. Please don't mind me wrong sir.

MANAGER: You don't have discipline at all. Ok. Ok. Hereafter, you should not come like this to an interview. Is it ok?

MANI: Ok sir. Would you like to interview me? I mean., Do you ask questions?

MANAGER: *(With wrath)* what is this new question Mr? Don't speak like over-enthusiastic and act like haphazardly.

MANI: Sorry Sir, I am extremely sorry.

MANAGER: Our Company is a finance company. I mean a Cash flow company. Do you know?

MANI: *(Having held his head high)* I know very well sir.

MANAGER: Therefore, I am going to question you about the „money matter".

MANI: Is it money matter? It's our matter sir. Why because, my name itself, Mani sir *(In Tami language, when the word, Money is pronounced, it has the phonological similarity with the Proper noun, Mani)* Hmmm. One minute sir! (*While speaking, he stood up and took a knife from his pocket and placed it on the table. Having seen that, the Manger trembles with fear).*

MANAGER: He yells.... Hey Knife, kn..ife., kn..ife., this is knife.

MANI: You have uttered it correctly sir. It is not an ordinary knife. It has been strongly made from pure steel sir.

MANAGER: (*with astonishment*). I don't need the history of knife. Why have you placed this on the table? Tell me.

MANI: Nothing sir. We are the descendants of 'Kattabomman'. Our people always have the knife with them. As I sat on the chair, it struck me. That's why, I took it and placed it on the table.

MANAGER: Oh! I see. I actually got panic. (*With hesitation*) Shall we start the interview?

MANI: Oh! Yes. with pleasure. If you ask simple questions, it will be feasible to give answers.

MANAGER: (*Staring at the knife*), There is no other way. By promise, I will ask only easy questions. Is it enough?

MANI: You have a golden heart sir.

MANAGER: Till the last time, the mind was like iron, now has melted and become gold...Hmm. Let me ask you a few questions. Say a few proverbs related to money.

MANI: Having taken the knife in his hand, a knife can jump a feet whereas money can jump even into the underworld.

MANAGER: Terrific proverb. Hmm... Next, please place the knife on the table.

MANI: Ok sir. Still three more proverbs are needed.

*(Places the knife on the table)*

MANAGER: No need... No need. The one proverb that you stated is equal to four proverbs. Ok. Next question. Do you know the value of US Dolor?

MANI: What are we going to do, having known that? Should I say certainly sir?

MANAGER: (*staring at the knife*), nothing like that. If you desire, speak. Otherwise, leave. Next question. What is the richest country in the word?

MANI: Why should we worry about the world? Just think about our country also.

MANAGER: Ok...Ok... Do you know who is the first richest man in India?

MANI: Sir. Please don't ask the name of the guy. I get the maximum rupture. While a large multitude suffers in country, he is the one who enjoys. Isn't it wrong sir?

MANAGER: Unless you desire, leave that question too. Ok ...One clarification?

MANI: Ya... sure. Please ask it generously.

# IS THERENT WAY IN THE EARTH?

MANAGER: May I know in which category should I ask you the questions?

MANI: Oh! Sure. If you ask questions related to knife, I will answer all questions like „„one cut giving two pieces".

MANAGER: Oh! my god. Don't speak about knife again, Mr. I have known about your credentials. By the by, let's close the interview with this. You shall leave.

MANI: Thank you so much sir. Can I get this job sir?

MANAGER: *(whispers)* God only knows it.

MANI: Even if don't get the job, that is not the issue. I like you so much. As and when I come to market, I will certainly meet you sir.

MANAGER: Is it?

*(Mani takes the bag and snake gourd in his hands)*

MANI: Then, shall I leave sir?

*(Forgets to take his knife)*

MANAGER: You have forgotten to take your knife...

MANI: Placing his knife in his pocket - *(with the touching tone)*

Sir.. Thank you so much sir.. I had actually tend to forget the symbol of my descendent. I don't know how to say thank you for reminding me. I will never forget you in my life sir.

*(After having moved to some distance, he returned again lifting the knife from his pocket)*

Sir, if it is useful to you, you please have it sir. I will buy a new one.

MANAGER: Hey... *(astonished)*. Oh! No. not required. It should be with you.
First, keep it inside.

MANI: Thank you sir. We leave temporarily, but meet frequently. Ok sir. Let me leave.

*(Leaves, having given royal salute for two times by stretching his body and leaves the spot mourning)*

At what price are the vegetables sold? The price is tomato is of gold. The price of snake gourd is of diamond. Yep.

MANAGER: ya..ya..

*(In the same way, sits on the chair)*

************************************************************

## SCENE - 3
**Locale:** Manager's Chamber
**Participants:** Manager and Raja.

---

RAJA: Good Morning sir!

MANAGER: Please, be seated.

RAJA: Thank you sir.
 *(Sits on the chair)*

MANAGER: Are you Mr. Raja?

RAJA: Yes, sir.

MANAGER: Where is your Bio-Data? Give it.

RAJA: *(Raja hands over the file to the Manager. He refers the same and converses...)*

MANAGER: Yep. You have done B A. In addition, you have been certified with type writing. Hey! Have you participated in the State Level Tennis Tournament? Good to see! By the by, shall we commence the interview?

RAJA: Ok sir.

*(By this time, the phone rings. The Manager speaks over the phone.)*

MANAGER: Hello... May I know who is speaking? What...*MD sir*, is it? Good Morning sir...Good Morning sir... *(Hurriedly)*

*(Instantly stands from the chair and confabulates)*

Ya sir. Only one vacant sir.

What...? Is the chap closed to you? What's his name? Ok sir. I take care sir. *(Chuckles).* Then sir...About my promotion? Hmm. will you look into the matter? Ok sir...Thank your sir. Thank you very much.

*(Manager hangs the phone and sits on the chair. He then, wipes his face with hand kerchief, in pursuit, looking at Raja. . . )*

Hey, chap! Are you ready for the interview?

RAJA: I am "already ready" forever sir.

MANAGER: *(Turning aside and murmurs)* why is the guy speaking indifferently? *(looking at Raja)* Ok. Ok. You know very well that our company is a finance company. Therefore, let me ask you a few questions about finance.

Yep. first is about robbery. That is., I want to test you how far you are familiarized with robbery? Is it ok?

Do you know the name of a "King of Robbery" who invaded our country for about 17 times and embezzled all the valuables from temples?

RAJA: Mahmud of Ghazni sir.

MANAGER: Brilliant...Excellent...Do you know the name of the person who is prime the reason for the advent of the British to our country as businessmen, looted all our wealth, and eventually ruled us, in particular, Tamil Nadu?

# IS THERENT WAY IN THE EARTH?

RAJA: Robert Clive!

MANAGER: Exactly Correct. Hmm… then, Can you please say the name of   the trending Hollywood glamorous actress who stole the hearts of her fans nowadays?

RAJA: *(with the frowning face)* I don't know sir.

MANAGER: Don't know? No issues at all. Has any damsel stolen your little heart?

RAJA: *(Taking some time to ponder)* don't know sir!.

MANAGER: what a lad you're!. A lad having not fallen in love is not a  *"man"*. Ok… *At least,* do you know, what do you mean by *stealing one's heart?*

*(Raja nods his negatively to show that he doesn't know.)*

Don't you even know that? Why are you so infirm in general knowledge. You respond to all questions as *"No"*. What do you know *then*? Tell me.

RAJA: Only one thing is *obviously* known sir.

MANAGER     : Tell me even *"that"*.

RAJA: I know that this is an interview for just *"eyewash"*.

*(Raja vacates the spot with wrath)*

MANAGER: *(with bewilderment)* Hey..Hey..chap..

**************************************************************

## SCENE - 4
**Locale:** Beach
**Participants:** Raja and Babu

--------------------------------------------------------

*(Raja is seated at the beach, having felt fatigue.That time, his pal Babu visits the spot)*

BABU: Hey...Raja!

RAJA: Hello! Come Babu.

BABU: what Raja? Why are you to be indifferent? Why does your face look like a *half-moon*? What's wrong with you?

RAJA: Nothing dude. You know very well that my father works in a mill.

BABU: What's up with that now?

RAJA: You know well that I have a younger sister at the marriageable age.

BABU: I know it. What's up with that now?

RAJA: The mill where my father works has been locked for about six months.

BABU: Ok... What for it?

RAJA: Our family has been in abject poverty. I haven't obtained any job so far. My father vehemently scorns me every day, saying problems of family. For the past one week, he scolds me a lot. I feel dismay in going home.

# IS THERE N'T WAY IN THE EARTH?

BABU: Are you being seated as life-disgusting only for this?

RAJA: What shall I do dude? I have participated in many interviews and I didn't get the job from anywhere!.

BABU: Are you still doing the idiosyncratic deed of participating in the interviews?

RAJA: What...! Do you want to say that I needn't go for any interview?

BABU: Why do you search the way for a city that doesn't exist? Why do you anticipate the rises of the Sun in the East?

RAJA: Dude, what do you want me to do, then?

BABU: You don't do anything. Follow me without uttering anything. I will make your problems to vanish in air.

RAJA: Where are you calling dude? Babu: Do you need job or not?

RAJA: Yes. Of course.

BABU: Money.

RAJA: Certainly, needed it, due.

BABU: If so, don't ask any question. Follow me.

*(Babu leads Raja accompanying him).*

*******************************************************

## SCENE - 5
**Locale:** Road
**Participants:** Babu, Raja and Chellapa

------------------------------------------------------------

*(Babu comes along with Raja on road. Raja's college mate Chellapa arrives at yonder. Chellapa recognizes the both of them. But, Raja and Babu cross by without noticing him. Babu takes Raja in to a secluded place. As soon as their departure to that spot, Chellapa gets into the entry of the place)*

CHELLAPA: (*Speaks in soliloquy*) why is he going with him? He is such a "different guy" ...Hmmm. Let him come. We'll enquire!


************************************************************

## SCENE - 6

**Locale:** Premises of Drug Trafficking
**Participants:** Raja, Babu and Madam

------------------------------------------------------------

BABU: Madam, he is my soul mate named, Raja. He has completed BA degree. He has tried for his job in many places and got frustrated. His dad randomly begins to criticize him. He is in the verge of disappointment towards his life. That's why; I have accompanied him to meet you. You are one who can eschew his dismay.

MADAM: *(Gently pats on the shoulder of Raja)* Come chap... come... Don't worry. I will sort out all your problems. I have established this group only for those youngsters who miserably failed in their life. The youngsters like you should be consoled. My objective is to create a reformation in the life of the youngsters.

Yep. Form today onwards, you have become one of the members of my group. Ok. You will have an assignment on the 5th of next month. I am going to assign the work to you.

RAJA: How much is the salary Madam?

MADAM: (*Giggles*) Ha...Ha... salary? If I give salary, that will not be sufficient for you. My practice is that I will fix rate for every assignment and offer you as salary. That's all. I have fixed twenty thousand rupees for this assignment

RAJA: Oh! twenty thousand rupees?

MADAM: Have five thousand rupees as advance!

RAJA: Madam… you didn't say anything about what the nature of the job is?

MADAM: It is just a simple task. This box contains the Ganja packets worth of Rs.50 lacks. This box has to be transported to a place which I am going to say.

RAJA: (*with anxiety*) Madam…Is it drug trafficking?

MADAM: Hey, chap why are you frightened like this? Did I ask you consume the drug? There are people who want to experience it outside. This product has to be transported to them. That's all.

RAJA: Madam, If I am caught by police?…

MADAM: You will not certainly be caught. I will offer you prudent techniques and strategies.

RAJA: If this news is publicized, people will think me in a different way?

MADAM: Raja…who are the people considering you wrongly? Can the people who criticize you get a job for you? Will the people who speak ill about drug trafficking show the right direction to you? Speak dear! Speak. If we fear, the society will strangle you being lethargically seated on you. If we have the courage to retaliate, the so-called society itself will subdue. Understood? Hmm... Raja? Don't unnecessarily confuse yourself contemplating this or that. Sharply come here on 5th Ok?

RAJA: (*Nods his head with a kind of hesitation.*) Ok Madam.!

*********************************************************

## SCENE - 7
### **Locale:** Road
### **Participants:** Raja and Chellapa

------------------------------------------------------------

*(Having received Rs.5,000/- as an advance from the Drug Trafficking Gang leader, while Raja came out, he astounded witnessing Chellapa standing at the entrance. After adjusting himself. . .)*

RAJA: Are you Chellapa?

CHELLAPA: Yeah! Raja. I am the same person.

RAJA: How many days have it become? How do you do? Where are you working?

CHELLAPA: I'm alright. Why have you come to this spot? Raja: I came to meet my companion.

CHELLAPA: Please don't mind of asking. Have you come to meet a friend or a fraud?

RAJA: Hey, chap...chill... what do you say?

CHELLAPA: I know him dude.! That guy Babu...his behaviour...his trade...I know everything yaar...Why did you go with him?

RAJA: Nothing serious yaar. I just came to meet him!.

CHELLAPA: Raja...If you truly have regards with me, and believe that I am your pal having care and concern towards you, you should explicate whatever happened here. Otherwise, leave it. Let me leave from here.

RAJA: What Chellpa?... Why are you so tensed? Let me tell you what happened here. After having completed BA., I tried my level best to get a job for three years of time. There were many intolerable problems at home. At this neck of the moment only...Babu...Hmmm. (*He explicates his pain and pangs through gesture*)

(*Having looked around, he whispers all the incidents towards Chellapa's ear with hesitation*).

CHELLAPA: I too intuited the same. Is it the matter? At this juncture, you should definitely meet with a person. Now itself, let me take you with him. Follow me!


************************************************************

## SCENE - 8

**Location:** Chamber of Nallasivam
**Participants:** Raja, Chellapa and Nallasivam

-----------------------------------------------------

NALLASIVAM: Come Mr.Chellapa? Be seated. Who"s he?

*(Raja and Chellapa are seated.)*

CHELLAPA: He is my college mate sir.
*(To Raja)* I'm working as a Manager in Sir's factory only.

RAJA: Greetings sir!

NALLASIVAM: Back at you. By the by, I'm Nallasivam. Your good name? Please.

RAJA: I'm Raja sir.

*(At this time, the telephone alarms and Nallasivam speaks over the phone.)*

NALLASIVAM: Hello! Nallasivam here. Oh! Are you Ramau? What happened? Have you received the contract? *(After a pause)* Very good. Have they agreed for our quotation? You have done a good job Mr.Ramu. I wouldn't be worried, even if the contract is not allotted to us. I earnestly appreciate that you have eloquently elucidated the quality of our tea powder and obtained the contract. I have deciphered so many times. I believe that you remember the same. We always opt the policy "Quality first and Profit is secondary". Then, you please make your presence in the party for sure.

*(Hangs the Phone)*

(*Looking at Chellapa*) Our buddy Ramu only spoke over the phone. Do you remember we were confabulating the one crore contract on tea power on that day?

CHELLAPA: Yeah sir. You were telling that we had many tough competitions.

NALLASIVAM: Yeah, yeah. We have eventually obtained that contract. Chellapa    : (*Gleaming*) Is it sir?

NALLASIVAM: Yep, Chellapa. By the by, why have you brought Mr.Raja to me? You didn't say anything about him.

CHELLAPA: He needs your guidance sir.

NALLASIVAM: Hmm. What sort of my guidance is required for him? Chellapa : Sir, It has become three years, since Raja had completed BA degree. He has relentlessly tried for jobs in many places but couldn't. Therefore, he accords that he wants to join in the "Durg Trafficking Gang". I felt pity about him. During that time, I had a deliberation of making him to meet you. That's why, I accompanied with him.

NALLASIVAM: Very good. The problem of Raja is unemployment right? Ok. I alone, need to answer for this. Mr.Raja, what's your age?

RAJA: I'm twenty-five years old sir.

# IS THEREN'T WAY IN THE EARTH?

NALLASIVAM: At present, I am a business tycoon. I have all sort of luxurious facets of life such as car, bungalow, property, money, jewels and servants. But, for about twenty-five years ago, my plight was totally vice-versa!

During that time, I was at your age. My dad was a rickshaw driver. He strived a lot for giving me education, in pursuit, I completed B.Com. Then, I also encountered the scenario of searching for jobs like others. I was wandering but, I was not able to get the suitable job. Two years rolled out like this.

Unfortunately, my father was in ailment. He couldn't drive the rickshaw. The back-up money in hand slowly began to vanish and we felt very difficult to get even the food. We had skepticism whether we will survive or not?

During that time, I attempted into a novel endeavor. I had prepared the tea in a large utensil and transported the same to the companies and some prominent localities using bicycle.

The family gradually began to sprout out with the profit and I began to accumulate the money. Eventually, I inaugurated a new Tea Shop in a nearby rented room.

The business in the shop slowly began to surge. During that time, I got the companionship of Mr. James, who is a dealer in supplying the tea powder to the tea shops. He interrogated me whether I can supply the tea powder to some places as his agent. I in turn, joyfully agreed.

In pursuit, the slow and steady growth has transformed me to be the owner of some tea estates and the proprietor of some companies.

Mr.Raja, I told you about my growth in a nutshell. This achievement had come from the right path and there were three fundamental notions for this. The first is self- "confidence", the second is "effort" and the third is "hard work" that's all Raja. There are plethora of paths in mending money in the world. One is through the "virtue" and the other is "vice". The path of vice will be glitteringly visible. On the contrary, everyone has to strive for tracing out the path of virtue which will be quite difficult to achieve.

You try to find an appropriate path. Unless you find the right path, you come and meet me after two months of time. Then, I will let you know what is to be done.

RAJA: (*overwhelmed with emotions*) Please pardon me sir. I was getting ready to select the wrong path without contemplation. After having listened to your advice, I have completely been transformed. Now, I will throw Rs.5,000 received from that anti-social group.

Now, my mind has become cleansed. I have been imbibed with new hope and confidence. I don't know how to say my gratitude to you.

CHELLAPA: Raja, you should not go to that faulty place. I will inform the police and let them all be grabbed. Then, you asked me earlier how to cite your gratitude. If you achieve to an ideal societal status, having chosen the appropriate path, it is more than enough and that is the succor that you offer to me. Ok?

*(Raja stands as a mark of respect towards him. Nallasivam pats on his shoulder).*

**(The End)**

**************************************************************

# 3. LOVE IN THE LAND

## DRAMATIS PERSONAE

1. MANICKAM     - Youth

2. SHANMUGAM - Manickam's father

3. LALITHA       - Manickam's lady love

4. SHANKAR      - Manickam's college mate

5. MUTHU         - Office mate

6. AMUTHA        - Manickam's neighborhood girl

**************************************************

## **SCENE - 1**
**Locale:** Home
**Participants:** Manickam and Shanmugam

------------------------------------------------------------

*(Having been seated at chair, Shanmugam is reading the newspaper. Manickam enters charmingly, having a letter in his hand.)*

MANICKAM: Dad!. . . an ecstatic news.

SHANMUGAM: What dear! Have you got any ransom from lottery?

MANICKAM: No dad! Nope! Bigger than that. You are going to reap the benefits for your sufferings.

SHANMUGAM: Hey! I am *perplexed*. Natter it in detail dear!.

MANICKAM: Dad! I have got an *offer* from "Star Finance Company" as an 'Accountant'.

SHANMUGAM: Is it Manickam? For the past few days, I was in ailment. I was not able to concentrate on our Salon Shop. I was thriving a lot how to lead our family. It is so fortunate that you have got this job offer at the right time. Do you know how I am relaxed? Ok. When have they asked you to join?

MANICKAM: Coming Wednesday dad! I am going to distribute the sweets to all my companions and neighbors dad!.

SHANMUGAM: Certainly, you need to do it dear! You buy and disseminate everything to them today itself. This morning, Amutha, a lass, from the next door came and she also deciphered that she too got an job offer from a company. She is a modest girl dear! Now, there is a speculation about a law which stresses that equal importance should be given to women like men. Is it true?

MANICKAM: Ya dad! Nowadays, many women are going for job. Even though they get emolument, they are not able to look after the husband and children, after the marriage. The children are reared up without having the so-called familial affinity.

SHANMUGAM: So, do you want to highlight that women should not go for job?

MANICKAM: Dad! *(in a mellow voice)* I am not asserting like that. The pains and pangs of a person are to ameliorate the family. I mean, those who are not able to look after their family shall avoid in going for a job.

SHANMUGAM: Ok dear! Have food, after taking bath. Let me go to shop and get back.

MANICKAM: Ok dad.


***************************************************************

## SCENE - 2
**Locale:** Railway Station
**Participants:** Manickam and Lalitha

------------------------------------------------------------

MANICKAM: Ma'am, is it your wallet?

LALITHA: Thank you. Thank you very much. Here, the wallet has not only money, but also some prominent receipts in it. The train was thronged by people. While getting down from the train, I missed. Thank God. As a good fortune, it has reached you. Had it been taken by others, it is doubtful to get the same from them. Is everyone as good as you?

MANICKAM: That's all right. Let me leave for now.

LALITHA: Hmm. You didn't say anything about you. By the by, what's your appellation?

MANICKAM: I'm sojourning at Periyar street. My father is Mr.Shanmugam. If it is said as "Shanmugam from Salon Shop", everyone knows about him in this vicinity!.

LALITHA: Then, where do you work?

MANICKAM: Recently, I have got a job offer. I am going to join as an Accountant at Star Finance Company from coming Wednesday onwards.

LALITHA: Oh! Kudos.. It's a renowned company. Sir, You are really lucky.

MANICKAM: What is about you? What are you doing?

LALITHA: I have completed B.Sc. I have been searching for a job till now. We are sojourning at Door No: 05, in Thiruvallur Street. My father is a retired Station Master at Railways. Is it your nearest station?

MANICKAM: Yeah. Even the next station has the same distance from here. However, it is more feasible to me.

LALITHA: So.. well, let's just say that we meet often.

MANICKAM: For sure. *(with hesitation) If* you don't mind, may I know your appellation?

LALITHA: It's my pleasure. I'm Lalitha. (*Giggling*). Ok then, Let me leave.

MANICKAM: *(slightly nodding his head)* Ok.

*(both of them departed in an opposite direction. After leaving yonder, both looked back at each other and left at the same time.)*

***********************************************************

## **SCENE - 3**

**Locale:** Office

**Participants:** Manickam, Muthu and Shankar

------------------------------------------------------------

*(While Shankar and Muthu are seated at Office, Manickam enters).*

MANICKAM: *(to Muthu)* Good Morning sir. I am Manickam. I have been newly recruited here.

MUTHU: Welcome, Welcome. Is that you? Be seated. That's your seat.

MANICKAM: May I know your good name please?

MUTHU: I'm Muthu. At the same time, *(Pointing at Shankar)* He is Mr.Shankar.

*(Manickam gives his hand with Muthu. Next, while giving hands with Shankar). . .*

MANICKAM: Sir. I think that I have already spotted you!.

SHANKAR: Oh...is it? Ya..I too have the reminiscence of your face!.

MANICKAM: Hmm. Did you study at Nandanam Arts College?

SHANKAR: Aye...then, you?

MANICKAM: I too studied over there. I completed the degree in 1991.

SHANKAR: Hey.. I got it. Were you Shankar, the secretary, 'Tamil Literary Association'?

MANICKAM: Ya..Correct. You?

SHANKAR: I am Gowri Shankar. He shortened my name as *Shankar.* Do you recognize me?

MANICKAM: Oh my goodness! Are you Gowri? How have you changed in this 6 and 7 years of time? How can I forget you? You were the one who scored the first mark in the college. How did you join here?

SHANKAR: I applied for this job last year, having seen a newspaper advertisement and I got the job immediately.

MANICKAM: Is it? Seeing you here is an unprecedented surprise for me!. Hmm. Then, are you married?

SHANKAR: Last year only, I got married. As I was not aware of your address, I was not able to inform. Sorry dear.

MANICKAM: That's all right. Where are you put up right now?

SHANKAR: I am sojourning in a rented house at Tambaram. By the by, are you married?

MANICKAM: As of now, *No* dear. I got the job now only. Hereafter only, I need to think about the other things.

SHANKAR: Then, How is your dad? Is your shop going well?

MANICKAM: Salon? Ok… but, now there are many varieties of hair idiosyncratic styles, having been followed. Dad is very orthodox belonging to the old age school. Hence, it goes in a slow phase.

SHANKAR: So what? You've now grabbed the job right? Wouldn't you look after your family?

MANICKAM: Certainly dear!. My first and foremost priority is to give vacation to my father. Ok dear. I'm departing to my seat.

MUTHU: Hmm. You have become companions. Now, I am the person who stands alone.

MANICKAM: What do you say sir? We, the trio, are good friends from now onwards.

MUTHU: Have you taken it seriously? I just kidded.

*(The trio laughs looking each other).*

************************************************************

# SCENE - 4

**Locale:** Railway Station
**Participants:** Manickam and Lalitha

------------------------------------------------------------

*(As Manickam walks by, Lalitha comes in front of him)*

LALITHA: Hey! Manickam. How do you do?

MANICKAM: I'm fine. What is about you?

LALITHA: I'm alright. Then, have you joined in the job?

MANICKAM: Oh... yes, I have joined.

LALITHA: How is your work going?

MANICKAM: My work is so interesting. As I have the close proximity with the public, I don't even feel the movement of a day Then, after having met you on that day, I couldn't meet you further.

LALITHA: My brother is aspiring for MBBS entrance examination. I have been guiding him. Hence, I couldn't move anywhere.

MANICKAM: Oh! Is it? *(looks at watch).* I have been waiting for a long time for train. It hasn't come so far yaar!.

LALITHA: Should you go immediately?

MANICKAM: It's not like that. I am always accustomed of being occupied at my seat 5 minutes earlier.

LALITHA: Are you so sincere to that extent? You are so peculiar *(with the bashful smile).* If the train is delayed, I will feel fortunate.

MANICKAM: Why do you say so?

LALITTHA: *(with the coyness)* then only, I can casually confabulate with you from the heart about certain things.

****************************************************************

## SCENE - 5
**Locale:** Home
**Participants:** Amutha and Shanmugam

----------------------------------------------------------

SHANMUGAM: Come, Amutha! Be seated!

AMUTHA: It's Ok Uncle!

SHANMUGAM: Have you in job dear!

AMUTHA: Nope Uncle! Nobody is there at home to look after the family. Even if I too go for job, I felt that I will not work out. That's why, uncle I had relinquished the idea of going for job.

SHANMUGAM: That is too correct!.

AMUTHA: Uncle, isn't he there?

SHANMUGAM: Are you talking about Manickam? I guess that he has gone for film. You too studied with him from school days onwards right?. Then, why are you giving him respect as *Avaru*, Ivaru*?*

*(In English, the word, 'he' is used as same to call out a person either with or without respect. However, in Tamil language, the same word is used either 'avaru' or 'ivaru' to denote respect and 'avan,' 'ivan' without respect).*

AMUTHA: *(with shyness)* we studied together only but I used to call him with due reverence. Uncle it's ok. Did you eat?

SHANMUGAM: I had it just earlier. Hmmm. Should I inform him anything, while he comes?

AMUTHA: I happened to see him reading a novel on that day. Had he completed the same, I thought that would have then borrowed the same from him.

SHANMUGAM: Let him come. I'll get it from him. What's the name of the novel then?

AMUTTHA: "LOVE IN THE LAND"

**************************************************************

## SCENE - 6

**Locale:** Office

**Participants:** Manickam, Shankar and Muthu

---------------------------------------------------------------

SHANKAR: Hey! Manickam. You were standing happily with a girl at the railway station. What was the matter?

MANICKAM: Shankar, please don't think it in the other way. Her name is Lalitha. We both are in sincere love.

SHANKAR: That damsel seems to be exuberant. How was she grabbed by you?

MANICKAM: Hey.. yaar! What do you *say*? Is she rat or a tiger to be grabbed? We saw, conversed, mingled, and loved each other. That's all!

SHANKAR: You are an ex-secretary for "Tamil Literary Association." That's why, you speak in a poetic diction. Who did express the love first? Is it you or she?

MANICKAM: We, the duo only. Why do you ask?
Shankar: I thought that you might have beseeched and cajoled her.

MANICKAM: Do you know Tamil Literature heralds that there is nothing wrong in pleading with a woman for love-making. The renowned the poet laureate Kannadasan has sung: "The man in love is a slave." Do you know?

SHANKAR: You have all the information in detail. So, it means that your love-making travels in the path of success.

MANICKAM: What's the doubt there? Like a growing crescent, it continues to grow day by day and every now and then.

SHANKAR: The reason for asking the same is that some of our people have started to fall in love. Then, they have been singing like *'Devadas* and I belong to the same clan.* That's why, asked.

*(*Devadas is a fictional Character, known by Indians. He miserably failed in love. So, whenever people quote someone who has failed in love, they make the reference towards Devadas).*

MANICKAM: Our love is so genuine. What did you think about Lalitha? Even if intimated today, she is ready to come out of her house to be with me forever. She is such a great lady love.

SHANKAR: Very good. Very good. Keep rocking. My wishes in advance. (*To Muthu*), Muthu sir, you didn't say anything regarding the love affair of Manickam.

MUTHU: *(with frustration)* you are all talking about love-making. I'm very weak in that subject. That's why; I have kept my mouth shut.

SHANKAR: Why do you *feel* so sir? How many movies have you watched so far? How many lovemaking shots are exquisitely shown? Even after that, if you say that you are feeble, how is it Sir?

MUTHU: I am also doing the love-making with a girl but, she's not uttering at least some sugar-coated words in love.

SHANKAR: Sir... *(with perplex)* you didn't say anything. Who is she sir?

MUTHU: She is none other than, my wife.

*(Shankar and Muthu place their hands on their heads, as a mark of disappointment).*

*********************************************************

# SCENE - 7
**Locale:** Home
**Participants:** Manickam and Shanmugam

------------------------------------------------------------

SHANMUGAM: Hey…Chap! Tell me, whatever I happened to know is true?

MANICKAM: What is the matter dad!?

SHANMUGAM: That is none other than, your love issue.

MANICKAM: *(with the trembling hand and biting his tongue out of fear)*

Dad!… (*with the mellow voice and speaks with the fragmented voice*) I… had a thought…. of informing you).

SHANMUGAM: Why are you blabbering something? Speak it clearly.

MANICKAM: I initially had a reflection of intimating the same to you.

SHANMUGAM: I guessed. I thought that you have forsaken me by simply assuming "Is he such a great person to be informed? Why should I inform this to him?"

MANICKAM: Nope dad! You go to the shop earlier in the morning and you come late from the shop at night. That's why, I didn't get the right time to inform the same to you.

SHANMUGAM: Hey...what do you bluff? Is it an international issue? Can't it be addressed within five minutes?

MANICKAM: Apart from lack of time, I had a hesitation to inform you. That's why, I had procrastinated the issue with a thought that it shall be intimated later.

SHANMUGAM: What you told is correct but, ignoring that you are beguiling that you don't have time, this and that.

MANICKAM: Ok dad! The cat has come out of the bag. Will you give your consent for my marriage?

SHANMUGAM: Hey! Chap. Are you doing this with your own consciousness?

MANICKAM: Why do you ask so?

SHANMUGAM: Will you ever develop an affair towards an upper caste girl? Do you know who are they?

MANICKAM: Dad! You are still in the ancient mythical school. Now, the concepts such as upper caste and lower caste have vanished. Everyone is equal.

SHANMUGAM: Don't simply say like that. Do you know even nowadays there are many commotions and aggressions in the village side in terms of communal clash?

MANICKAM: She is the one who is not concerned with community.

SHANMUGAM: Do you know one thing? 50 years ago, we were not supposed to go near the streets where the upper caste people lived. If we ever happen to meet them, then we will need to tie the towel at the waist as a mark of respect, and we need to bow our head. Do you ever realize these sorts of sufferings that we have undergone?

MANICKAM: That's what I told you, now the society has changed a lot.

SHANMUGAM: How did it change? Was just changed just like that? It was actually reformed by the strenuous endeavors and sacrifice of the social activist Periyar E. V. Ramasamy.

MANICKAM: I do agree dad! She has her heart and soul towards me.

SHANMUGAM: Do you know that if there were no Periyar in this country, we couldn't have lived in this land as human beings. After a prolonged struggle, you have got this job. Instead of focusing on the job and thereby developing yourself, you are deviating yourself in terms of love. I don't like it to the core.

MANICKAM: Haven't you heard the maxim that Love is divine

SHANMUGAM: I don't know whether it is celestial or mathematical. Whatever I wished to express, I have expressed. Then, it's your wish! That's all.


*********************************************************************

## SCENE - 8
**Locale:** Park

**Participants:** Lalitha and Manickam

-----------------------------------------------------------

MANICKAM: Honey! It got delayed a little. Did I make you to wait for a long time?

LALITHA: That's not like that. Even there is a pleasure in waiting for something.

MANICKAM: *(Giggles)* if so, I will always come late hereafter. Is it ok?

LALITHA: Hey darling! Nope yaar! I simply uttered a word just for formality. You're very rapid and it is like, * If I ask you just to be Sesame, you are ready to become 'Sesame Oil' itself. *

MANICKAM: I went to a shop in order to select a gift for you. That's why, it got delayed.

LALITHA*: (with curiosity)* what honey? Is it for me? *(blushes with smile)*. What's that gift? Unveil it to me.

MANICKAM: Nothing so serious honey! I was able to buy this watch only for you. Do you like it honey?

LALITHA: Oh! fantabulous dear! You have really chosen it well. How is it dear? It closes to my heart.

MANICKAM: Having imagined your colour and texture of your glossy hand in my mind, I have chosen this. That's all honey!

*(He ties the watch on her hand)*

LALITHA: Thank you very much dear!

MANICKAM: I only need to utter the notes of thanks to you.

LALITHA: What is it for?

MANICKAM: First, it is for offering your unconditional love to me and also for providing me an opportunity to wear the watch on your tender hands.

LALITHA: I guess that you are exaggerating.

MANICKAM: It's the truth, not a hyperbole.

LALITHA: It seems that if given an opportunity, you will write poetry.

MANICKAM: I will write not only poetry but also an epic.

LALITHA: Manickam, we met only a few days back. I have never dreamt that our love will get developed like this within a short span of time.

MANICKAM: It is stated that every seed needs its own soil for its evolution. Say for example, Alluvial soil is for banana tree. Black soil is for Cotton. Likewise, you have been captured by me.

LALITHA: *(Cajoling and with a mellow voice)* Am I caught? Can't I escape ever?

MANICKAM: *(Holding the palms of Lalitha)* you *can't* escape. Can a moon be separated from welkin? Can an ocean be separated from the land?

LALITHA: I am a spinster dear!

MANICKAM: That's why I told you that you can't move away from the confinement of my heart.

************************************************************

# SCENE - 9
**Locale:** Home
**Participants:** Shanmugam and Manickam

-----------------------------------------------------------

*(Shanmugam reads the newspaper)*

SHANMUGAM: Prime Minister visits abroad. Gold rate surges.US does bomb blast attack again in Iraq. They will never leave. *(Turns the Paper).* Karnataka rejects the plea of Tamil Nadu in releasing the water. The renowned Company is shut down. The famous finance company named "Star Finance Company" is being permanently closed from today onwards. (*with shock*), what...? Has the company been closed? Manickam! Hey, chap Manickam come here.

MANICKAM: What baba?

SHANMUGAM: Just read this dear.

MANICKAM: What's the matter baba? *(with astonishment)* Have they closed the company?

SHANMUGAM: Why have they done like this suddenly?

MANICKAM: Wait for a while dad! *(He scans the newspaper).* Some of the officers of the renowned finance company named, "Star Finance" have executed a huge scam in terms of lending. The company suffers with the severe financial crunch due to that. The company is being closed temporarily from today onwards. The reopening date will be announced later. *(folding the newspaper).* Dad! It has become like this! *(with utter frustration).*

SHANMUGAM: It seems not sure about their reopening. Lot of people are working in the company.

MANICKAM: Dad! just analyze this issue. The flaws committed by the people with higher order seriously affect the people with the lower order. These people neither know nor responsible for anything. For so many days, I strived a lot in getting this job. Eventually, all my endeavours went in vain.

SHANMUGAM: Hey dude! Nowadays, righteousness and sincerity have simply diminished in our country.

MANICKAM: It hasn't diminished dad! rather I think that it has become void. Yeah! *(with resentment)* once again, the job searching portal begins.

SHANMUGAM: Ok. Let it happen, as it is to happen. Don't worry for anything and try for your next career.

**************************************************************

### SCENE - 10
**Locale:** Home
**Participant:** Manickam

------------------------------------------------------------

*(The mobile of Manickam rings. Lalitha speaks over the phone.)*

LALITHA: Hello! Manickam. I had a thought of meeting you but, I don't know how to express it to you in person. That's why, I called you over phone.

MANICKAM: *(with swiftness)* Lalitha...What happened? What is the matter?

LALITHA: That's ...one of our relatives from the US came home seeking alliance with me. He was interested in me. As my parents and relatives had compelled me, I was not able to retaliate. Please forget and forgive me.

*(Latha disconnects the mobile. Drops of sweat sprout at the face of Manickam.)*


***************************************************************

## **SCENE - 11**
**Locale:** Home
**Participants:** Manickam and Amutha

------------------------------------------------------------

*(Manickam rapidly goes for consuming the venom. By that time, Amutha guards him arriving on the spot.)*

AMUTHA: Dear! What sort of heinous act have you done?

MANICKAM: Why did you come here Amutha? You please go away from here and come later.

AMUTHA: What did make you to consume poison? Tell me.

MANICKAM: Why are you bothered about that? Get lost from here.

AMUTHA: You still didn't answer for my question.

MANICKAM: I have thousand problems and I need not tell those things to you. Would you like to move away from here or not?

AMUTHA: Let me get lost from here. I too will go to the shop for procuring the poison. Let me too get a bottle of poison and consume the same.

MANICKAM: Why should you conk?

AMUTHA: For the reason that you're going to die.

MANICKAM: If I perish, why should you too die? Are you either my lady love or wife?

AMUTHA: Both for sure.

MANICKAM: Amutha, what do you *mean*?

AMUTHA: From the day of my childhood, I have the affection towards you and I will do the same till my last breath.

MANICKAM: Why are you blabbering like this all of a sudden? Are you insane?

AMUTHA: I am uttering all these things with my full consciousness till now.

MANICKAM: Then, you are gabbling, as if you have affection towards me.

AMUTHA: I'm seriously having crush towards you. When I wanted to reveal the same to you, I came to know that you were in love with Lalitha. In pursuit, I buried my love at the bottom of my heart. I desired that you should lead a happy life with a girl with whom you are in love. Eventually, that too hasn't happened.

MANICKAM: How do you know it?

AMUTHA: When you had the confabulation with Lalitha over phone few minutes earlier, your phone was in loud speaker mode. Hence, I was able to listen. I grieved contemplating will there be a girl like this? And I was worrying too much reflecting that you should not go to any ill-fated decision. Whatever I thought not to happen, has happened now. As a good fortune, I came here at the right time. Give me that bottle.

MANICKAM: I can't...I shouldn't live here after.

AMUTHA: Why should you die just like that? You are propagating that it is love but, I tell you that girl didn't have affair with you at all.

MANICKAM: How...How do you say so?

AMUTHA: Had she really loved you, will she ever get a reflection of marrying another person? Answer me. She loved you for the sake of your job and money.

MANICKAM: *(with astonishment)* what do you *mean* Amutha?

AMUTHA: Ya.. I'm telling you the reality. When you had a good job, she pretended as if she was in love with you. When you lost the job, she left you just like that. That's all.

*(Manickam bows down his head and stands with reticence).*

Let me explain you clearly. It is injustice to sacrifice your life for a girl who doesn't love you. You still have a lot of responsibilities to be accomplished. I wouldn't quibble you that you should accept me but, my humble plea is that you shouldn't unnecessarily lose your life for the life that doesn't exist. *(after a while)* Let me leave for now.

*Amutha walks out...*

MANICKAM: Amutha...just wait...*(after a while)* Every word that you uttered is true. I believed a silhouette as veracity till now. I was wandering all the places believing the bogus as legitimate. I was moving in the wrong lane and you are the one who made me into the right path. You are the one who have unveiled my eyes of knowledge which were closed earlier. Hereafter, I *will* not die and I *will* not die forever!

AMUTHA: *(with overwhelmed feeling)* Thanks a lot dear. Ok. Let me leave for now.

MANICKAM: Amutha... just a minute. Let me ask you one thing. Will you do a favour for me?

AMUTHA: For sure!.

*(Manickam walks adjacent to Amutha)*

MANICKAM: Will you be a *companion* to me for the whole life?

AMUTHA: Hey, honey!  I belong to you *only!*

MANICKAM: Amutha!

*(Both of them join their hands together)*

**(The End)**

**************************************************************

# 4. WILL THE CAPABILITIES FAIL?

## DRAMATIS PERSONAE

1.  KUMAR           - Youth, Writer
2.  SHANTHI         - Kumar's sister
3.  RANI             - Kumar's lady love
4.  FATHER          - Kumar's father
5.  MOTHER         - Kumar's mother
6.  PRODUCER     - Film Producer
7.  DIRECTOR      - Film Director
8.  ASSISTANT     - Director's Assistant
9.  OFFICER        - Officer from film company
10. AGENT           - Film Agent

******************************************************

## SCENE - 1
**Locale:** Home
**Participants:** Mother, Father, Kumar and
Shanthi

------------------------------------------------

MOTHER: Shanthi! Did you wake up your brother? Have coffee. Give it to him. He doesn't spend his time at home during day time. He rests only at night. If asked, he speaks the philosophical words like *this* and *that*.

*(Shanthi brings the coffee to Kumar, but he is at sleep).*

SHANTHI: Bro.... Dear bro... wake up. Time is 7 am. Wake up.

KUMAR: *(doing the pandiculation)*, Hmmm. What...? Has it become 7 am? You could have woken up little earlier. Couldn't you?

SHANTHI: Have you forgotten dear bro.? When I came here by 6 o' clock, you only insisted me to come later and wake up. Ok. Ok. You please wake up quickly and have a cup of coffee. Dad has gone to rest room. If he comes now, he will chide at you stating why he is sleeping for a long time.

*(Kumar is seated on the bed and receives the coffee).*

KUMAR: Shanthi, you are the only person in our home to support me. Even if Dad looks at me, he is exasperated. Having the fear towards dada, Mama won't retaliate for anything.

*(Kumar sips the coffee)*

SHANTHI: What happened to the screen play of your film project bro.?

KUMAR: I have been to many film companies. They all told some lame excuses and informed me that they won't take it into consideration. Today, I have the plan of visiting to another film company.

*(Kumar returns the empty coffee tumbler to Shanthi).*

SHANTHI: Bro... I have a serious inclination of making your story into a film.

*(Dad hastily arrives into the hall).*

FATHER: *(shouts at wife, by calling her name)* Lakshmi... Lakshmi.

MOTHER: *(Comes out instantaneously).* What... what?

FATHER: Let me leave. Hmm... Where is Shanthi?

MOTHER: She has gone to offer a cup of coffee to Kumar.

FATHER: Yeah! That King* *(Hyperbole)* really suffers without getting coffee.

MOTHER: Why dear? *(in a mellow voice)* Why are you talking like this?

# WILL THE CAPABILITIES FAIL?

FATHER: You are the only person, placing the crown on that vagabond. Ok. Ok. It is getting delayed. Let me leave.

*(Father leaves. Mother's face is so dolorous)*

MOTHER: *(Gets into Kumar's room).* Have you ever thought about our family? Your dada strived a lot and offered you education. Your sister has to be married in a due course of time. Don't you have any sort of remorse for it?

KUMAR: Mama…as advised by you and dada, I don't like to be placed in accompany where I have to toil till the end of life to earn money. *Writing* is my preferred profession. I am aimed to be recognized as a renowned writer.

MOTHER: Ok. Let it be. Don't you like to earn at least to fulfil the financial needs of the family?

KUMAR: One day, my writings will be acknowledged and I will be getting many bucks for my writings.

MOTHER: Whatever I say that you're not going to listen. I am only unnecessarily shouting to dry my throat.

SHANTHI: Why are you getting wrath towards bro.? Everybody has their own desires and ambitions. In the same way, bro. has the passion towards writing. Why do you accuse him?

MOTHER: Have you also begun to speak in favour of him? Whatever I wanted to convey, I have conveyed. Then, it is thug between you and your father.

## **SCENE - 2**

**Locale:** Film Production Company Office
**Participants:** Kumar and Producer

------------------------------------------------------

*(A board named 'PRODUCER' hangs in front of the chamber)*

PRODUCER: *(Looking at Kumar who stands near the door),* what do you want?

KUMAR: *(Getting inside),* Good Morning sir.

PRODUCER: Come! Please be seated.

*(Kumar is seated at the chair)* Yeah! Tell me.

KUMAR: I'm Kumar sir. My writings have been published in journals and magazines, since last two years.

PRODUCER: Oh! Ok. What can I do for you?

KUMAR: Sir, I came to know that you were giving chances to the new comers. I have drafted a screenplay and wanted to show the same to you.

*(He submits the file to him)*

PRODUCER: Dear chap! You have come here without knowing the background information. I'm not finding fault at you. You are at the young age and you don't have enough experience. Cinema is like an Ocean and if you want venture into it, you need have a lot of experience. Is it clear to you?

# WILL THE CAPABILITIES FAIL?


KUMAR: I have drafted this screenplay, having contemplated for a long time. If you go through it, you will definitely incline it.

PRODUCER: Dear chap! I guess that you don't get what I'm trying to say. Cinema is a big deal. Those who are in the field of cinema have offered me a lot of screenplays and I have got totally perplexed, having reflected on those stories. Why are you coming and disturbing during this time?

KUMAR: As I have the writing experience in journals and magazines, I have drafted the screenplay which can be accepted by the public and can successfully run in the theatres. Sir, you should read it once at least.

PRODUCER: Oh my god! Dear Chap! My time is getting wasted. Like you, many people are marching every day towards film companies with an advent desire towards movie. If I am addressing all of them every day, I then need to close the company and become bankrupt. First, you try to understand one thing. Writing something for a journal or a magazine is entirely different from writing something for a movie. Don't get confused with both. Continue your passion towards writing in journals and magazines. This is your file. Have it.

*(Returns the screenplay file)*

KUMAR: *(Standing from the chair)* Let me leave sir!


**************************************************

## SCENE - 3
### **Locale:** Park
### **Participants:** Kumar and Rani

---

KUMAR: Rani.... Has it become very late after your arrival... honey?

RANI: You used to come at least one hour late from your promised time. Having calculated the same, I came here and it has got adjusted.

*(both of them giggles)*

KUMAR: What shall I do Rani? I strive a lot to be on time any spot. However, it misses out.

RANI: I have a reminiscence of reading somewhere that the writers can't promise to maintain their time.

KUMAR: You are true Rani. As writing is associated with imagination, and the mind of the writer concerned becomes amalgamated with the writing, certain things are not to be accomplished on time. Then, have you applied for leave at office or permission?

RANI: Permission only. Did you meet anyone today? Any special news?

KUMAR: I have decided to go for a new company tomorrow. Wherever I go, people treat the newcomers in a different way.

RANI: Don't get frustrated for anything. Try for something with confidence. Is it ok?

# WILL THE CAPABILITIES FAIL?

KUMAR: Rani... I know that effort and hard work is the base for victory. However, when I ceaselessly face the failures, my mind becomes fatigue.

RANI: Honey...you will definitely need certain time and situation to explore your skills. The stars can winkle, only when the welkin becomes dark with clouds. The same has been stated by great scholars. Do you know that?

KUMAR: You're absolutely correct Rani. I'm ready to wait for the *right* opportunities, but dada becomes very angry towards me. He is continuously pestering me to join in any job. Ok. Let it be. You told me that you wanted to say something.

RANI: Two days back, suddenly they all started speaking about my marriage. I guess that my mama had gone for a wedding last week. During that time, one of our distant relatives had asked for an alliance with me. Mama told that to me. I had insisted her that let her not speak about my marriage at least for one year, but they are all elderly people and marriage is a prominent factor for them. They are all quiet this time. When it comes for the next time, I really don't know how to manage the situation.

KUMAR: When are you going to disclose our love-making to your parents?

RANI: I need to disclose it, when the situation favours. If your efforts are succeeded, it will be favoured for us. Is it right?

KUMAR: Certainly. What you say is centum percentage correct. My dear honey, Rani.

RANI: Then, Kumar, we have a cultural extravaganza at our office on coming Wednesday and you should take part in the function. I came here today to inform the same to you. You should come for sure. Ok?

KUMAR: Next Wednesday? ... (*thinking for a while*) Ok. I will come for sure.

RANI: *(looking at the watch)* Ok. Let me leave.

KUMAR: You could have something and leave...

RANI: Nope! Dear Kumar. Let me leave.

KUMAR: Ok.

**************************************************

## SCENE - 4
### **Locale:** Home
### **Participants:** Kumar, Shanthi and Father

-------------------------------------------------------------

FATHER: (*yells*) Shanthi.... Shanthi

*(Shanthi comes near her father)*

My dear little princess! What is about that sluggish chap? I'm talking only about the writer. Has he woken up or still sleeping?

SHANTHI: Dada! Brother has already woken up and he has been writing something.

FATHER: You ask him to come here, informing that I am calling.

*(As Shanthi informs him, Kumar arrives to meet his father)*

KUMAR: Dada! Did you call me?

FATHER: Hey! *(raising his voice)* What're you thinking in your mind? Do you wish to go for any job or not?

KUMAR: *(with hesitation)* Dada! I have drafted a new screenplay.

FATHER: Yeah! *(sarcastically)* It seems that *you have really done a herculean task of writing a screenplay.* Discard everything. Go to our hometown and look after farming. At least, you will earn some bucks. Understood?

KUMAR: Dada! While Mama, Shanti and you are sojourning here, how can I go to home town alone?

FATHER: *(Metaphorically)* Is affection pouring, having pierced something towards us from this *Lord*? *(Screams with wrath)* You aren't fit enough for even a single penny. Why do you need have affection towards us? Do you ever know what sort of job are your friends doing? Hmm. This place doesn't suits you and you better shift yourself to our village.

KUMAR: *(in a mellow voice)* Dada, I'm striving to submit my screenplay to a film company. Once it is finalized, I will then shift to our home town.

FATHER: What?... Is to be finalized?... *(anger is at peak)* Will you go, only if it is finalized? You, the *dumbass...* *When will the moustache grow on the face of an aunt? *When will the people start calling you as Uncle? Don't speak like an eccentric man. Listen what I say.

KUMAR: Dada!... Please give respect to at least my aspirations.

FATHER: You, the blockhead! *(A native proverb)* It seems like *a person who is not able to trap a hen, claims that he can show the way to heaven, by simply claiming at the sky. Everything happens, as the fate written on your head. Is anyone in our family ever experienced into cinema?

KUMAR: Dada! It is a superstitious belief that the job done by father should be done by his son. Leading the life through wood cutting, Abraham Lincoln, could achieve the designation of

'President' in the US only through his meticulous skills.

FATHER: I don't need to listen to those cock and bull stories. Listen! I have been giving you free food. Hereafter, it will not be given. I will give you a week of time. You try to get a job in between otherwise, go to your village with all the bags and baggage. I make it very serious. Don't forget.

*************************************************************

## SCENE - 5
### **Locale:** Park
### **Participants:** Kumar and Rani

---

*(Kumar has been brooding over bowing down his head. Even though Rani stood near him, he didn't notice her)*

RANI: *(gently pacing her hand on him, calls)* Kumar…

*(Kumar raised his head and looks at her).*

In what a deep contemplation are you engaged? It has become two minutes, after my arrival.

KUMAR: Pardon Rani…. I didn't notice your arrival… By the by, please be seated.

*(Rani seats near with him)*

Hm…. Then, I couldn't turn up for the function at your office. I'm really very sorry.

RANI: That's ok. Leave it. Why are you state like 'once in a blue moon'? Any problem?

KUMAR: Everything is problematic here due to money.

RANI: Is there any problem due to money?

KUMAR: Ya..honey. Dada is pestering me to join in any job that too in a week of time.

RANI: If it is not possible in a week?…

WILL THE CAPABILITIES FAIL?

KUMAR: If not, he asks me to go to my native village.

RANI: *(with astonishment)* Is it for village? What sort of job are you going to do there?

KUMAR: What else? There is no way other than doing agriculture there.

RANI: Have you given your consent? Would you like to go to the village?

KUMAR: I know agriculture but, I don't aspire to go there with my present mindset.

RANI: You could have openly enumerated this issue in detail to your dada, right.

KUMAR: I told him that I am at present working on my screenplay and once it is finalized, I will move to my village but, he doesn't give an iota of chance to listen to my words. He is very adamant. He has spoken everything like *a single cut giving two pieces (Native Proverb).*

RANI: Hey dear! *(with frustration)* Why has it become like this?...

KUMAR: It seems that this is called destiny, "Man proposes and god disposes."

RANI: Then, what's the next step dear?

KUMAR:  That's what, I called you to provide a solution for this issue.

RANI: Shall I try to get a job for you by getting the succor from my friends?

KUMAR: Rani.., I don't like to get these sorts of jobs working at office. It doesn't work out for me to do a job at any time, having been seated at a single place for hours together under the purview of officers with lot of terms and conditions. You do understand my mindset right?.

RANI: *(sighs)* Hmm…you want to be an independent writer but, people of your family ask you to be confined in an office. Do you see the difference of opinion of people living in a family?

KUMAR: Yeah! honey. The flower rose and its thrones are in a same creeper.

*(The situation becomes tranquility for some time.)*

RANI: Kumar…I have got an idea.

KUMAR: Tell me. Let me see, whether your idea at least helps me.

RANI: That is, I will offer you a particular sum to you and you pretend your family that you are working in a company and offer the same to them.

KUMAR: Sorry Rani. I utterly don't like this idea. My mind will not agree falsely claim your hard-earned money, as if it is earned by me.

RANI: What's wrong in striving either you or I? Why do you differentiate both?

WILL THE CAPABILITIES FAIL?

KUMAR: No...No... I don't differentiate. I staunchly believe that there should there should be always solidarity between words and deeds. Therefore, you totally ignore this idea.

RANI: Then? What's next?

KUMAR: After pondering over a lot of time, I could arrive at a conclusion. I should work hard for this week in terms of my screenplay issue. Unless it turns out well, I will then need to go my village.

RANI: *(with frustration)* What're you saying?... I guess that you're talking something, having totally forgotten that I'm here with you.

KUMAR: Why are you in a hurry? Did I ever tell you that I am going to sojourn at the village permanently? At this juncture, I should have to go to village just to pacify Dada.

RANI: Kumar... In my family, they are seriously discussing my marriage. If you're at least here, we can disclose our love making in a cogent manner. If you go to native place, then in what ground will I be able to convey this? You yourself tell me.

KUMAR: Whatever you say is right Rani but, my plight of life is like this.

*(Rani bursts into tears)*

Rani...What's this? Why are you weeping? Don't I have grief in leaving you? Tell me.

RANI: Have one thing in your mind... Unless you marry me, I will not survive in this world.

KUMAR: What Rani?... Why are you talking like this?

RANI: If I think that you are shifting towards your home town, I really feel terrible.

KUMAR: Do you know one thing? Our so-called literatures proclaim that lovers should not lose their hope, during this sort of tough time.

RANI: It shall be pronounced like this in literature, as it is bound on imagination....

KUMAR: Yeah! It's purely imagination..., but the experiences of life have become imagination and thereby, have become literature.

*(Rani bows down her head. Stillness prevails there).*

*(Kumar lifts up the face of Rani and consoles her).*
Look, Rani...Don't worry about anything. You should cultivate your mind thinking, that all that happens is for good cause...Ok?

*(Rani is without uttering a word)*

Is it ok?

*(After some time, Rani nods her head, showing the sign of consent).*

***********************************************************

## SCENE - 6

**Locale:** A Film Production Office
**Participants:** Director, Assistant and Kumar

------------------------------------------------------------

*(Director imaginatively converses showing his two hands, having checked the angles of the shot. Assistant follows him uttering the words 'yes sir'... 'yes sir'. They didn't notice the arrival of Kumar.)*

KUMAR: *(after a while)* sir...sir....

DIRECTOR: Who are you? What do you want?

KUMAR: Sir... Are you Mr.Nandagopal, the Director?

DIRECTOR: Ya..ya... I'm only. He is my assistant Mr.Madhana Gopal. By the by, what's the matter?

KUMAR: I'm Kumar sir.

DIRECTOR: Whoever you shall be, what is the benefit for us? Why do you come and disturb during this neck of the moment?

KUMAR: I'm so sorry. Did I disturb you sir?

DIRECTOR: Ya...It's a very big disturbance. Do you know that we were searching for the angle position of an important scene? You have totally collapsed everything.

KUMAR: I'm extremely sorry sir...I'll come and meet you later sir.

ASSISTANT: Do you even wish to come and disturb later? That is not needed. You can explain in detail now why and what for you have come here, you shall then leave.

KUMAR: I'm a writer sir. I have drafted a screenplay for a film. That's why; I wanted to show the same to you sir.

*(Soon after his statement, Director and his Assistant chuckle each other.)*

DIRECTOR: Hey, little chap... How many of you have come forward like this? Even though we all have crashed our heads, confused and wasted all our energy, we are not able to assimilate a story. How is it possible for you to impregnate a new story all of a sudden?

KUMAR: Sir... I have already drafted the stories in the journals and magazines. Having gained the experience there, I began to write the screenplay for the movie.

ASSISTANT: If you simply write two stories either in a journal or a magazine, should you then come to film industry? Why are you so greedy? Understand a fact that you can't write the script for the film.

KUMAR: Sir..., please do read my screenplay at least once... You will like it for sure.

DIRECTOR: *(Sarcastically)* Hey, chap...Do you know that what do you mean by a script? Do you know how many different varieties are there in shots? Do you know that what is screenplay? Otherwise, do you know that what is 'Direction' at least?

# WILL THE CAPABILITIES FAIL?

ASSISTANT: In the present time, sir plays the role of Director. Do you know how many people has he met and how many kinds of stories is he telling so far? If he thinks now, he can illustrate a script and make you in a different way. *(To Director)* Is it right sir?

DIRECTOR: *(with some stumbling)* yeah! yeah! You need to realize my potentials Dear... Let me begin to narrate the script to you. You listen carefully...

*(To Assistant)* You too...

ASSISTANT: Ok sir.

DIRECTOR: *(with gestures)* A Highway in the middle of the forest, Midnight 12 o'clock, thick night.

ASSISTANT: *(To Director)* sir... It seems to be the same story that I narrated it to you on that day.

DIRECTOR: *(whispers in the ears of Assistant)* Let's think about the ownership of the story later. Keep your mouth shut. *(looking at Kumar)*... Hmm...There is no light at all in the street.

KUMAR: That's what you told earlier that it was a thick night... Then, how can be there light?

DIRECTOR: What yaar? It seems that you're bypassing me... Light illumines to be an iota at yonder and this is supposed to be a long shot.

ASSISTANT: Wow! Wow!... You are meticulously explaining sir.

DIRECTOR: The next can be a medium shot. Our protagonist stands near the road with a suitcase...

ASSISTANT: Brilliant...awesome...

DIRECTOR: Then, the face of protagonist at a medium level close shot. The sweat has bloomed like little pearls on his face with the background score of winds rattling.

ASSISTANT: Is there any strange element such as the arrival of ghost sir?

DIRECTOR: Idiot. As it is a rainy season, the jolting sound of the wind is heard.

ASSISTANT: Is it? What is next sir?

DIRECTOR: The visual which was in the shape of an iota, comes closer. Now, it is clear that it is a Maruthi car and this can be shot, using a crane.

ASSISTANT: Do we need to use crane sir?

DIRECTOR: Shut up. You don't have enough experience because, we don't need to show the other parts of the car such as front, back tires and body. That's why, we shot it using crane.

ASSISTANT: You have a master mind sir

DIRECTOR: Thank you. Now, we shall show the *hands* of the protagonist, using a close shot.

ASSISTANT: Why sir? Has he got any injury in his hands?

# WILL THE CAPABILITIES FAIL?

DIRECTOR: Dull headed fellow! The protagonist waves his hand to stop the car. Do you understand?

ASSISTANT: Ya.. got it sir...got it.

DIRECTOR: My goodness... The car stops.

*(He leans on the chair)*

*(To Kumar)* How is the screenplay?

KUMAR: What you have told is not a screenplay, rather a scene sir.

DIRECTOR: *(Instantly straightens his posture)* What...? Do you criticize my screenplay? No chance is for you hereafter. Hmm...leave...stay away.

KUMAR: I came here thinking that it's a reputed company. Now, I understand that why you have established your office near a Mental Hospital. Let me leave.

*(Kumar leaves the premises)*

DIRECTOR & ASSISTANT: *(in a single voice) Ah!...*
*(a sign of dismay)*

****************************************************

## SCENE - 7

**Locale:** Road

**Participants:** Kumar and Film Agent

-------------------------------------------------------

*(As Kumar walks by, the film agent persuades Kumar).*

AGENT: bro...bro...wait for a while.

*(Kumar turns back)*

I'm Ekambaram, an Agent.

KUMAR: Is it?... What do you need sir?

AGENT: All right... The question I need to ask you that you ask me.

KUMAR: I don't understand what you speak...

AGENT: Didn't understand?... Ok... Let me make you to understand. Are you wandering to get an opportunity in a film?

KUMAR: Yeah! sir... How did you notice that correctly?

AGENT: *(smiling)* That's Ekambaram! Your face bubbles with the inclination towards 'Art' bro!

KUMAR: Is it?... Thank you sir...

AGENT: Oh!... my goodness. Have you grasped it?... I'm Ekambaram, the Film agent.

KUMAR: Is it sir?...

## WILL THE CAPABILITIES FAIL?

AGENT: Then, do you have your album ready?...

KUMAR: Album! *(with excitement)* Why is album required for me sir?

AGENT: What bro.?... You seem to be an innocent chap... Are you anticipating a chance, based on your album?...

KUMAR: Nope sir... I don't ask for any chance for acting. I'm trying to offer my screenplay...

AGENT: Oh! Are you a writer? Having perceived your personality, I thought that you were trying for acting.

KUMAR: *(blushes)* Is it sir? While I studied at college, I was acting in miniature drams but, I don't have any interest towards acting nowadays. I have the passion only towards writing...

AGENT: So what?... It may come like this or it may come like that in cinema.... Why not, it may sometimes even come in any way.

KUMAR: Once again, I don't understand what you try talk sir...

AGENT: That's agent, Ekambaram! Initially, it may be Greek and Latin to you. Once you are accustomed for sometimes, you will obviously understand everything.

KUMAR: Is it sir?...

AGENT: Yes bro... What I wanted to say, people came for acting in cinema have become *Directors* and people came as writers have become *Actors* later. That's why, I told you that it may come either this or that.

KUMAR: Oh! Is it?

AGENT: Do you come under this or that category?

KUMAR: Sir... I want to submit my screenplay.

AGENT: Ok. You come under this category... *(thinking for a while)* Ok. You shall submit... No issues.

KUMAR: *(with gleaming face)* To whom shall I submit sir?

AGENT: *(after a while, self-proclaiming)* Neither the Producer nor the Director is without knowing the so-called Agent, Ekambaram.

KUMAR: Sir...If so, please make an arrangement with someone to submit this screenplay.

AGENT: Even though I know everyone, I am reflecting that who will be the closest to your successes.

KUMAR: Thank you sir...

AGENT: Don't offer your words of gratitude. When your screenplay is published as cinema, we shall have the other formalities. Ok?

KUMAR: Ok sir.

## WILL THE CAPABILITIES FAIL?

*(Ekambaram ponders over for a while, having placed his fingers on his forehead closing his eyes).*

AGENT: Ok... Coming Wednesday is an auspicious day... Let me take you to a company. Be ready with sharp 7o'clock with your screenplay.

KUMAR: Ok sir.

AGENT: However, you have unfortunately met me. Henceforth, you will have a good time.

KUMAR: *(smiling)* Thank you sir. Thank you very much.

AGENT: Then, bro... you need to some arrangements, before we submit the screenplay on Wednesday... *(with hesitation)* A sum of Rupees Five thousand is required. If you offer that sum tomorrow, it will be beneficial. Ok?

*(Kumar is confounded)*

KUMAR: Sorry sir...I don't have money.

AGENT: Ok. Will you have at least three thousand rupees?

KUMAR: I don't have money at all...

AGENT: Then, how does your screenplay turn into a cinema bro.?

KUMAR: It's Ok. Let me leave...

*(Kumar leaves the spot)*

AGENT: *(Looking at Kumar who walks by).*

Bro. while you get money, come and meet me without forgetting. Ok?

131

*************************************************

## **SCENE - 8**
### **Locale:** Home
**Participants**: Kumar, Father, Mother, Shanthi
and Film Company Officer

-----------------------------------------------------------------

*(Kumar is ready to move to the native village with bags and baggage).*

KUMAR: Shanthi...let me leave.

SHANTHI: *(To father)* What Dada?... should brother go to native village for sure? Unless my brother is here, I feel boredom Dada.

FATHER: You feel boredom. Do you ever know that how am I being hooked with many problems? Ok...All these trivial issues will be sorted in a short span of time...

KUMAR: *(To Mother)* Mama, let me leave.

MOTHER: *(with grief)* Kumar...As soon as you reach, do send the letter. If you come across any ailment, inform to grandma. She will offer home remedies. Don't forget to apply oil and take bath on Sundays. Don't burn the midnight oil. Have food on time. Ok...then...

FATHER: Hey...Is he going for army? You are making a long list.

MOTHER: We have only a single male child. I feel really grieved that he sojourns alone at the village.

FATHER: He does not stay alone rather he goes to spend his time with grandpa, grandma, paternal uncle and aunty. Do you understand?

MOTHER: I do agree. Even if you have thousand relations, will they ever look after him like his father and mother?

FATHER: Is he a new-born child? They will take care. Don't worry.

MOTHER: What do you talk dear? You speak without any care and affection.

FATHER: Look. Affection is more increased during separation. Do you know one thing? If you are with money as backup, the so-called affection will persuade you. Got it?

MOTHER: Being a macho, you speak whatever you want to speak but, how will you ever understand the pain and pang of my tummy which has delivered him?

FATHER: What do you talk about? Is he going abroad? As soon as the leave announcement of Shanthi in just a four-month of time, we are going to meet him at the village. Why do you feel so remorse? Yes...dear...get ready...otherwise, you'll miss the bus.

KUMAR: Ok. Dada! Let me leave.

FATHER: Ok. Dear...

WILL THE CAPABILITIES FAIL?

*(Kumar gets ready from home, after bidding a bon voyage to Mother and Shanthi. During that time, a stranger visits the house)*

FILM COMPANY: Is it the abode of Mr.Kumar?
Officer

FATHER: Yes. It is...By the by, May I know who are you?

OFFICER: I'm from *"Mutamil Movies Film Company"*... *(To father)* Mr.Kumar?

FATHER: *(Pointing out Kumar)* He is my son, Mr.Kumar.

*(Officer exchanges his hand with Kumar).*

OFFICER: Sir...our boss has decided to shoot a movie with your screenplay. He has sent his car for taking you to office immediately.

KUMAR: Sir...I neither visited your company nor submitted screenplay over there.

OFFICER: The matter is entirely different. Do you remember that your short story was published in a magazine two months ago?

KUMAR: Ya... Even the Editor of the magazine called me in person and offered the encomium stating that many people wrote the letters of appreciation for that short story.

OFFICER: Our boss has chosen the screenplay. I have come here, after getting your address details from office of the magazine.

KUMAR: Oh! Is it?... It is just a one page short story sir.

OFFICER: My boss told me that the entire script of the film is being concealed in the gist of one page short story. Our boss has decided, if you visit there

and sign in the agreement today, the *Pooja* can be performed in the next week. Ok. Shall we leave?

MOTHER: Wait...wait for a while. Have a cup of coffee and leave.

OFFICER: Thank you so much ma'am. I had it just now. When I visit next time, we will have a sumptuous lunch. Ok. It seems that someone from your family departs to native. You have made everything ready with bag and baggage.

FATHER: *(struggles and stammers to speak)* That is actually nothing. I have to leave to my native for executing a job. Ok. You accompany with Kumar. *(Calling out Kumar)* You go along with sir.

KUMAR: Then, Dada! ...What...I?

FATHER: We'll see to it later. You depart with sir immediately.

OFFICER: What Kumar? Do you have any other job?

FATHER: That is nothing. He was actually ready to come with me near the bus stand. That's why, he asked. Am I a child? Wouldn't I go alone? Ok. Kumar...You please leave with sir.

WILL THE CAPABILITIES FAIL?

KUMAR: *(Bows down his head and chuckles)* Ok, Dada.

OFFICER: *(Looking towards the trio-Father, Mother and Shanthi)* Ok. Then, let me leave.

*(Officer and Kumar leave the spot).*

FATHER: I haven't recognized the potentials of my son. I have wounded his heart in many ways. Yeah! He is really a skillful person.

SHANTHI: Yeah! Dada. You just see how he is going to earn the name and fame in future.

*(All the three laugh).*

**(The End)**

************************************************************

# About the Author

AR. Arul Selvan was born on 1961. He retired from India Post Department and resides with family in Chennai. He has been writing in Tamil more than 30 years. His writings were published in magazines, broadcasted through Radio and telecasted by Television. Books with collection of his Poems, Short stories, Articles and Plays have also been published.

Email: writerararulselvan@gmail.com

www.ingramcontent.com/pod-product-compliance
Lightning Source LLC
Chambersburg PA
CBHW040804120726
48005CB00012B/1298